I am proud of you for accepting your gift. Everyone won't like what you have to say but you call it like you see it. (Literally)

~ Robert (Bob) Bell

I was so drawn to Sara. She is such a sweet, humble person, and I was amazed at what she came up with, things she could not have known.

~ Tim Hensen, Curator Adams, Tennessee Museum

As a Bell descendant, I knew something happened to the John Bell family in the early 1800's, but couldn't explain it. After working with Dr. Sue and Sara on this project, I am a true believer. The defining moment was when Dr. Sue asked, "Is there a Nancy Jane in a wheelchair connected to the Bell family?" And I did know. In this book, Dr. Sue and Sara clarify questions and unknown secrets about the Bell family.

~ Sharon (Bell) Hamilton

Through the Eyes of Angel Leigh

Dr. Sue Clifton

with

Sara Dulaney Pugh

BEAR SPIRIT PRESS

Bear Spirit Press
ISBN-13: 978-1-77115-999-9

A Bear Spirit Press Second Edition April 21, 2022
Cover Photos by Jessica Kell

Dedication

To my children LeighAnna and Randyn, I dedicate this book to you in hopes that one day when you read it, you will realize how important it is to ALWAYS be yourself and let God lead your way.

To my parents, thank you for loving me unconditionally.

Lastly, to Sue. If it wasn't for you, I wouldn't be able to share my voice and my heart with the world. I am thankful the WAY led me to you.

Sara Dulaney Pugh

Acts 2:17 (King James Version)

And it shall come to pass in the last days, saith God, I will pour out of my Spirit upon all flesh: and your sons and your daughters shall prophesy, and your young men shall see visions, and your old men shall dream dreams:

Foreword

**"Keep an open mind and an open path and the
WAY will find you!"
Dr. Sue Clifton**

In January 2015, I found myself on another whirlwind trip. This time it was to my favorite destination Alaska where I hoped to share the Northern Lights with my friends Hilda and Gayle. Witnessing this ethereal spectacle at just this time would be truly momentous even though I had been blessed many times observing her majesty Aurora dancing during the eight and a half years I had lived in this great state a few years ago. This trip was to be commemorative, scheduled just ahead of the release of my latest novel *Under Northern Lights*, Book II in a series under contract with The Wild Rose Press and my seventh book published.

Time to witness the Aurora was running out. Our eight-day stay was coming to an end, and only a faint cloud of green had shown itself. That was a couple of nights earlier while in my old home village of Manley Hot Springs. Our last day before our flight home was drawing to a close, and desperate measures had to be taken if the mission was to be accomplished.

"One last chance!" I announced as we three sat in our hotel room, our long faces etched in gloom over the prospects of having to leave the spectacular Last Frontier without seeing the magical lights.

"It will cost us to go with this photographer who is also a tour guide. But he's the best there is and takes amazing videos of the Aurora. It will be worth it." I added this as my closing argument.

The vote was three to nothing in favor of spending the money even though our cash flow was now at a slow, thin trickle, and our credit cards were teetering on "Busted by Damn!" But our gambling had paid off too many times during our senior adventurous years to go chicken now. We would take this last challenge to see the Aurora Borealis! I took out my cell phone and made the call.

"I'm not really taking a tour group out tonight since I'm videoing a UAF (University of Alaska) research rocket being sent into the Aurora," the videographer/tour guide told me. My heart dropped, landing around my ankles as my glance fell on the thrift shop Alaskan down coat and white bunny boots I'd purchased specifically for the grand finale.

"But if the three of you don't mind the distraction since my main focus has to be on videoing the rocket, we can pick you up at your hotel around 10:00 tonight." I'm sure he could feel my gigantic smile on the other end as it pulled my heart back in place.

That night, away from the stifling city lights and a good distance out of Fairbanks city limits where real Alaska begins, we disembarked from the tour van finding ourselves under a beautiful clear, star-laden sky—at a hearty forty below (-40 degrees Fahrenheit). We stood like frozen sci-fi characters barely able to move, swaddled in layers of thick down jackets and snow pants covering sweatpants, sweaters, long johns and two pairs of wool socks. Heavy snow boots further anchored us in the deep snow, and thick down gloves covered our fingers still screaming, "Frost bite!" Only our eyes showed, making us look every bit like the tourists from Mississippi we were as we waited and watched looking heavenward for what seemed hours. Then after a brief sprinkling of color powdered the sky, it happened…

God spread his hands in one giant sweep and the sky transformed into three-dimensional green and yellow curtains that undulated across the heavens opening on to a stage more magical than anything Disney or any computer-animated movie studio could ever produce! Across the flickering array of starlight gone mad, Aurora, madam of the night, drew her celestial wand and expelled multicolored flashes of awe for her earthly audience of three. As she danced, her shimmering silk gown infused more hues and more movement until the whole sky rolled in and out like a tumultuous sea, a kaleidoscope of colors that hit heaven's shore bouncing back and replaying over and over. Chartreuse smiling dinosaurs swirled and bounced over our heads like a herd of giant balloons breaking free in a Macy's Thanksgiving Day parade. Even the face of God appeared, testing us for comprehension of the Divine miracle of nature we were being allowed to witness. Tears cut icy trails down our cheeks as we hugged each other staring up at the incredulous supernatural display. Energy emitted from heaven warmed our bodies and recharged our souls giving each of us the ultimate sensation of being totally complete.

But the real disbelief came the next day when the photographer emailed his best group shot of us under the heavenly illumination. Something out-of-world swirled its paintbrush in the sky over us, a precursor to wonders and enlightenment that could only be heaven sent—just for me!

For months, I used the photograph as my Facebook profile picture, at book signings, presentations and every occasion to show how once again, "The WAY had found me!" Kay, a friend of mine, told me emphatically, "That don't just happen!"

But on the night of July 1, 2015, this latest piece of evidence validating my tried and true Code for Living proved to be only partially true. Yes, the WAY had found me that night in Alaska, but did it stand only for SUE, or was it a foreshadowing of the girl I was to meet five months later? This girl would prove to be every bit as mesmerizing as the Aurora and far more enlightening. On that night in July, I showed her my profile picture under the Aurora. After scrutinizing it, she looked at me, smiled, and said, "Oh! S for SARA!"

Through the Eyes of Angel Leigh is Sara's book, and I am but an instrument set in her OPEN PATH to share in revealing to the world her narrative of coming to age and coming to grips with "being different." It is Sara's story of realizing how God meant for her to use her gift for the good of others, and it is a retelling of real life true stories of Sara's encounters and the messages she has been chosen to deliver.

As you read Sara's story, you are sure to ask yourself: Can messages really be sent from beyond earthly life? Can these messages be communicated through human vessels put on earth by God, rather than by the Devil as many believe, for the purpose of comforting loved ones left behind and overburdened with excessive grief? Can the gift be used to answer age-old questions still haunting family members generations later?

If after reading the last page of this book, you doubt the truth of these miracles, or if too many questions overpower your thought processes, just "Look to the heavens!"

Dr. Sue Clifton

Photo by Ronn & Marketa Murray Photography
www.ronnmurrayphoto.com
(Fairbanks, Alaska; left to right: Hilda, Gayle, & Sue)

Part One

Sara

Chapter One

Medium?

Call time is 5:00 PM at the cemetery. The producer and film crew will meet you there.

The quick text from the researcher for the production company illuminated my phone screen increasing my excitement for my first TV appearance. This was the culmination of a long Skype interview a month or so earlier concerning the many paranormal investigations I had conducted at the grave of Elizabeth "Betsy" Bell Powell who is buried just down the road from my home in Yalobusha County, Mississippi. Betsy was the main character, or should I say "victim", in the historical legend about the Bell Witch. The story began in 1817 and is claimed by both Tennesseans and Mississippians who, like me, find the old story intriguing, the stuff of which great ghost stories become legends with more truth than myth. In addition to almost two centuries' worth of articles and books written on the subject, the twentieth and twenty-first centuries have seen numerous movies released on the Bell Witch, some more realistic than others.

Regardless of how many times and how many ways Betsy's story has been told, the subject remains shrouded in mystery and unanswered questions, and I for one, am totally addicted, feeling an inexplicable camaraderie with Betsy.

And now here I was about be part of a television series based on the Tennessee Bells and their "Family Trouble!" The five part series is to air on one of the major TV channels in the fall, and I owe my small part in the series to my good friend Pat Fitzhugh for suggesting the film studio get in touch with me. Pat is from the Nashville area, is an author, and is an expert on the Bell Witch phenomenon not to mention being a fellow ghost hunter.

My part in the TV series amounted to one night of filming in the old, historical, and very isolated Long Branch Cemetery where I was to actually be part of an investigation at Betsy's grave just like I have been doing for the last three years. Along with myself, a medium from South Mississippi was being brought in to see if she could communicate with Betsy or any member of her family buried in the cemetery.

Yeah, right!

Call me a skeptic, but I had been told on a few occasions, usually by the "medium" in question, while ghost hunting all over the United States, that she or he was a person who could conjure up and communicate with the dead. But I had never found one who I considered credible or who told me anything other than what was printed on pamphlets or websites advertising these hotels, prisons, historical houses, vacant hospitals and insane asylums, etc., as "paranormal hot spots." But even though I thought the medium business to be for the most part deceiving, I would act as if I believed and let the night run its course. Besides, even my husband doesn't believe in the voices (EVP's or Electronic Voice Phenomenon) I have caught on my camcorder during investigations so my own credibility was in question.

I do not consider myself a professional paranormal investigator, but then —there really is no such thing as a professional paranormal investigator. No license or credentials is required, and probably the only thing an investigator might do to fit the definition of a professional is to charge for his/her services. Paranormal investigating (ghost hunting) is my hobby, one of many, and a means of researching for my paranormal mysteries, one of the genres I write as an author. When researching for this book, I looked up professional paranormal investigator credentials and found what I already knew—anybody who calls themselves a paranormal investigator can be a paranormal investigator. The same might be said of a medium, but just as in being designated a paranormal investigator, the proof is in the—uh—proof.

At almost dusk, the medium arrived at the cemetery. The pretty young blonde woman flashed me a sweet smile as she got out of the car and headed toward me, and I immediately warmed to her. Perhaps she could communicate with the "almost dead" since I am a senior citizen.

"I'm Sara." She gave me a big meaningful hug.

"I'm Sue." I immediately felt the night would not be a complete loss even if the spirits chose not to show. I liked Sara.

We walked over to Betsy's grave and began chatting, not small talk but conversation like we had known each other for years. This was good. I would be able to introduce her to the guys in the episode as my friend when the filming started without it being an untruth.

"When I was on my way here, I kept getting a name, and I need to know if it means anything to you." Without hesitating, Sara began in a soft, pleasant voice as she asked, "Do you know a Nell, or a Nellie, or maybe a La Nell?"

A bit taken aback, I replied, "Yes, I know one person named La Nell." Where was Sara going with this?

"Oh, good, then this must be for you." She smiled in sweet relief, seeming to be a little unsure, or perhaps, uneasy giving me, a stranger, a message from someone who died three years ago.

I showed no great reaction because the La Nell I knew was not a member of my family, not directly anyway, but Sara had grabbed my interest. The La Nell I knew was a wonderful woman, one I had always enjoyed being around and hearing from her would be something—if this were real.

"Did anyone connected with La Nell have surgery recently?" She added the question as if she was unsure, or perhaps she wanted to give me time to process before disclosing more.

"Yes," I replied tersely, thinking maybe she would give me the rest of the information without my helping her. She responded with another question.

"Do you know a Lee or a Lynn?"

My attempt to show little or no interest was no longer possible.

"Lee is my daughter-in-law, the daughter of La Nell." Again, I gave only the bare information necessary. I…was…good!

"There must have been complications, or the surgery was hard because La Nell's message is, 'Tell Lee I was there with her, holding her hand the whole time.'" Sara watched gaging my reaction.

My attempt to remain stoic failed as tears filled my eyes, but in the back of my mind I was still the skeptic. Could she have gone back three years and seen posts about La Nell's death on my Facebook page? But I was not FB friends with this girl and knew there was little on my timeline about La Nell's death. In fact, neither Sara nor I knew each other's name until the night of the filming. As if Sara were reading my thoughts, she continued.

"La Nell was a tall, sophisticated woman, really pretty with short gray hair, wasn't she?"

"Yes." I confirmed the description and knew this could not possibly be gained from Facebook or my personal website. My skepticism faded as the lump in my throat grew lumpier.

"Oh, yes, one other thing La Nell said to tell Lee."

I looked into the girl's eyes and waited, somehow sensing she was about to drop the proverbial bomb, giving the true validation I needed to confirm her credibility.

"La Nell said to tell Lee she still wears her makeup." Sara's eyes twinkled as if she knew this was the kind of information I needed, a personal touch of trivia.

At this point, tears filled my eyes and overflowed, forcing me to wipe them. La Nell was a beautiful woman and never went out without her makeup perfectly applied, especially her lipstick. Some of her final words spoken before she was no longer able to talk, were to Meredith, the oldest granddaughter she and I share and adore.

"Don't forget my lipstick!" La Nell spoke softly, peeking through eyelids soon to close for the last time—at least in this world.

"Yes, Sassy (La Nell's grandmother name). I promise I'll put it on you." A few days later, Sassy was taken out of Lee's house on her way to the funeral home. But even though she had passed from her earthly home into eternity, she was going with her lips brightly shining, like the beautiful, endearing mother and grandmother she would always be. Meredith had kept her promise.

I did not relay this conversation to Lee, but later that night,

Sara sat by me and added, "La Nell wore dark red lipstick, didn't she?" It was then I told her La Nell's dying words to Meredith.

That night, Sara delivered messages to two other people taking part in the show we were filming. They, too, were told things only their loved ones could know, messages to ease their grief.

While we were eating late that night, Sara walked quickly to the car she had ridden in and returned in just a minute and handed me a notebook.

"I wanted to show you where I scribbled La Nell's message. I always do this so I won't forget anything. This bottom part about the dark haired man is another message so just ignore that." Sara held the page out, and I took a picture of the notes so I could show Lee when I gave her La Nell's message.

The next day I told my daughter Niki, an even bigger skeptic than I was, about Sara's message to Lee. Niki searched my Facebook pages going way back and concluded there was no way Sara could have known the personal information about La Nell and Lee. Sara doesn't even have a computer at the moment since hers has been broken for a while, and she relies only on a cell phone.

I told Lee about the message from her mom on the phone the day after the filming. She was at work in the middle of an audit and had to contain her emotions, but I could tell she was on the verge of tears. Lee told me about being put at ease just before going to surgery. The pre-op was performed by all male nurses who in Lee's words "though proficient in their work, were not as tuned in to the emotional needs of the patient (her) as female medical personnel, especially female nurses generally are." Lee knows since she is a registered nurse and administrator over a home health and hospice agency, not to mention she is a sweet, gentle person known for showing compassion. Lee said just when she was feeling extremely frightened, a very kind female nurse entered the room, spoke softly, and held her hand.

"It was exactly what I needed, and a sense of peace and calm came over me. Do you think it could have been my mom with me through the nurse?" Lee asked the question, and I agreed it was possible, but regardless, the proof was in the notes Sara had hastily written, her validation of her ability to receive communication from those who have passed on.

As I added the photo of Sara's note page to the end of this chapter, I noticed a word scribbled in the margin. Chills ran from the top of my head to the bottom of my bare feet under the dining room table where I was writing.

"Way?"

Once again, the WAY had found me!

Sara is for real!

La Nell and Lee
One week before La Nell's death

Sara's Note

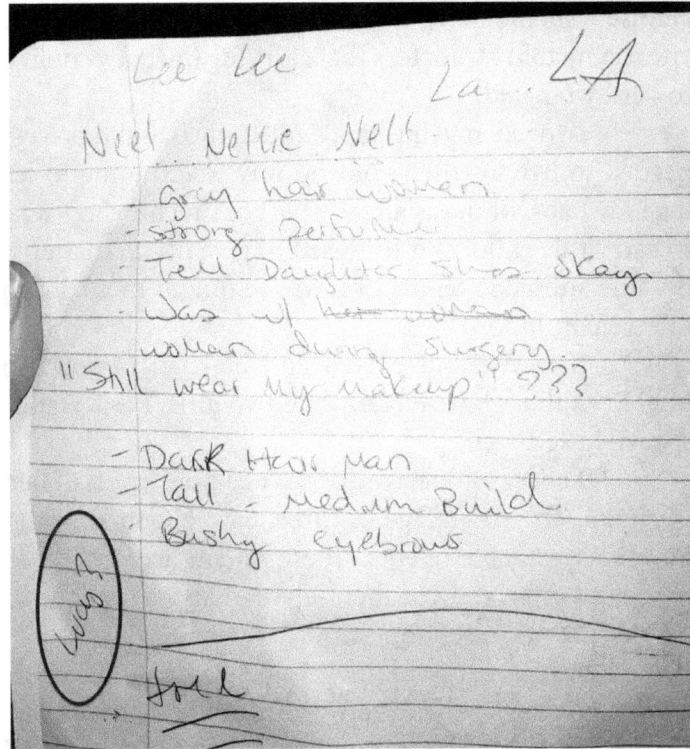

Chapter Two

"Stinky Poo Poo Man"

Sara is the youngest of three girls, the baby, and has always been adored by her parents, Denise and Randy. During our first interview, Denise explained how she knew Sara was special even when she was still in her womb.

"When I was three months pregnant, I began having big troubles and was told I would never carry this baby full term." Denise remembers vividly the emotional turmoil she went through after being told by doctors that carrying the baby could be dangerous to her own health.

"I loved my husband and two daughters very much and needed to live for them, but no way was I going to let the doctors take my baby who was already part of me, of who I was. I was going to carry this child, and I refused to give up no matter what." Denise became animated telling of how she fought mentally and physically to save her unborn child.

"I prayed and prayed and had faith everything would be fine. Even though we already had two girls, I told Randy, 'This is my special little angel.'"

Denise would have no idea just how "special" her angel would be, but at the young age of three, Sara began showing exceptional and unexplainable talents. These talents were not confined to the home but often showed themselves in a surprising manner in every day settings in the community.

Denise, Sara's mother, told her daughter about something which happened when she was little, about three years of age. The toddler wandered away from her mom at the grocery store, and Denise, a vigilant mom, panicked with the realization Sara was no longer beside her. Immediately, she began searching for her beautiful little girl with long blonde hair, the description fitting many little girls targeted by child kidnappers and molesters. Denise found Sara hugging the legs of a woman, a stranger, who was crying by the time Denise reached her little girl.

"Oh, I'm so sorry if my little girl upset you." Denise reached for Sara's hand horrified of what she must have done to make this lady cry and yet was relieved Sara was okay.

"Oh, no!" sniffed the lady. "It's all right. She came up to me singing a nursery rhyme song, my daughter's favorite, and the one I sang to her as she lay dying in my arms. Then your little girl smiled and told me, 'It's okay. Sally says 'it's okay, Mommy!' My little girl's name was Sally, but I've never seen your little girl before and don't know how she knows this."

Denise knew at this moment Sara was different, but she never relayed this story to anyone other than Randy. Denise's own mother and father, being devout Christians, had not allowed any discussion of such paranormal goings-on by any family member with this sort of gift or experiences thinking it against Christian doctrine and Biblical teachings. But lack of talking was not to keep Sara's abilities, her gift as she refers to it, from resurfacing again and again.

Soon after the grocery store incident, Denise and Randy found an older house in south Mississippi, a house they wanted to make a home for their three beautiful little girls. Randy put in a bid on it, a low bid but one he knew they could handle. Besides, the bidding tended to be low for some reason, probably the fact people had moved in and out of the house for years with no explanation as to why.

Good fortune came their way, or so they thought, and Denise and Randy made the house a home as soon as their bid was accepted and the bank had, without question, given them the necessary loan.

The two older sisters left for school each day, leaving Sara and her mother to enjoy the new house. Sara seemed to love the long hall best of all, the unending track for her Big Wheel (*reminiscent of the movie made from Stephen King's The Shining*)—that is until things started happening!

"I was wishing dishes at the sink one morning and felt a cold hand on the back of my neck." Denise put her hand around her neck to demonstrate. "Thinking it was Randy pulling one of his usual pranks, I turned real quick trying to catch him, but no one was behind me. It gave me the creeps, but I just dismissed it as my imagination playing tricks on me. But then Sara started acting strange. This was right after we started taking down a wall, after peeling off the layer of paneling to get down to the original wall."

Denise goes on to explain how Sara was sleeping with her one night soon after renovations had started, and the toddler woke up pointing and screaming, "There's a man!" Denise was unnerved by the episode, but she and Randy looked all over the house and found no one.

"The next morning, Sara and I walked the girls to the bus stop like we did every day." Denise explained. "When we got back inside our house, I locked the door behind us. Again, Sara started screaming, 'There's a man!' Oh, my gosh! I'd locked my baby and me in the house with a strange man! I grabbed one of Randy's golf clubs and held it up ready to swing as I went room-by-room searching but finding nobody. Sara refused to walk, so I had her on one hip and Randy's golf club clutched tight in my other hand. All of a sudden, Sara pointed and yelled, 'Mama, that man—you step on that man!' I looked down but the floor was empty."

As Sara balanced precariously on her mother's hip, she started talking about the "stinky poo poo man."

"What does the stinky poo poo man look like, Sara?" Denise held her daughter close to console her.

"Santa Claus—not big Santa Claus—little like you, Mama! Poo poo stinky man!" Sara turned up her tiny nose and pinched it together with her fingers.

Sara continued to talk about "stinky poo poo man", and one day soon after, Denise asked a neighbor who had lived there for a long time, if she knew who had lived in the house originally. The neighbor told her an old man, a hermit with a long beard lived there for many years until he died but people didn't see him out much. She said this was fine with them because the old man never bathed and smelled like he had used the bathroom on himself.

"I couldn't believe my little girl had described the man to a T. I walked through that house angry and yelled for that old man to leave my family alone! That night, Randy and I put that paneling back up as fast as we could."

"Things were going real good with us until we moved in that house," Randy added. "Then everything fell apart. I lost my job, our money dwindled away, and we ended up moving."

Next, Randy and Denise moved to "Grandpa's land, the old homestead" and bought a really nice doublewide Buccaneer, top of the line, but Denise said Sara never felt comfortable here either.

"I always slept with my door open and the hall light on. I was terrified of the dark and scared the whole time we lived there even though the doublewide was new." Sara explained. "Mama and Daddy lived on the other end of the house, and I felt insecure being so far away from them. No one ever saw me leave a room in that house unless I was running. It felt like someone was always behind me."

But it was here in the Buccaneer, the same Source that made her feel different, provided her with a means for solace, comfort and coping—most of the time.

Chapter Three

Blue Bubbles

Beginning elementary school was a big event for little Sara like it was for other children, but by the time Sara reached third and fourth grades, she struggled with what she was able to see, hear, and feel. Many times she was frightened and wondered if she was crazy. Her protective parents did not want her to talk about her seeming ability to communicate with those who had passed, especially to anyone outside the family.

"Don't talk about what you see, Sara, or people will think you're crazy!" Her parents often warned. They worried about their little girl being ostracized within her school and community or thought of as weird or crazy. But as Sara became more aware of her differences from other children, God provided her with something to comfort her and give her pleasure in her unnatural world.

"When I was ten, I would lie in my bed and watch bubbles in the ceiling, hundreds of bubbles that would follow me around." Sara smiled as she told about this childhood memory. "They became my imaginary friends and comforted me. I was never alone as long as they were there. I called them 'lost souls' and could see little faces in each of them. Sometimes, I would call Daddy in there and say, 'Look, Daddy,' but he couldn't see them. They were mostly blue but sometimes would change colors, and I could move my hand around in the air, even in swirls, and they would follow it. After the bubbles appeared, I had a dream about a big bubble rolling, filled with all the faces of people I knew. The bubble would suck up people's souls as it rolled but it wasn't scary. Now I know they were orbs, but I always called them bubbles and was never frightened by them."

Sara went on to tell me her three-year-old son Randyn now sees bubbles of his own. She often hears him giggling and sees him trying to catch or pop them. Her nine-year-old daughter LeighAnna also sees people others do not see. Sara says she learned from the fears of her own parents and knows they were just trying to protect her, but she will be open and supportive of her children's differences if they continue to develop.

"Most important, LeighAnna and Randyn will be made to feel comfortable and able to talk about their differences and still feel normal." Sara nodded her head asserting her intentions as the mother of children with possible differences like hers.

At this point in the interview, as the bubble talk came to an end, I found my cold chills had grown their own cold chills. I stopped the tape recorder and turned to the Kindle app on my cell phone where I searched for a book I had written several years ago, a paranormal mystery entitled *Keeper of the Lambs*, published by MuseItUp Publishing. My audience of Randy, Denise, and Sara seemed captivated, not knowing what to expect as I read aloud the following excerpt:

Bar None, Idaho
The Present

> *In the far corner of the room, the bubbles swirled in a thin blue mist, as if they were trying to move undetected. Inside the mass of blue, a smaller white circle of motion spun faster than the blue bubbles. K.C. looked at Wy and pointed.*
>
> *...*
>
> *K. C. could do nothing but stare in amazement as the blue engulfed her and Hank. She was in the midst of a swirling sea of aqua, surrounded by what seemed like hundreds of spherical fish with slanted eyes and tiny mouths, each bubble fish keeping time to Hank's playful notes (on the piano). In the midst of the sea, a tiny ripple of white twirled like a ballerina...*
>
> *...*

Next the blue bubbles appeared as if propelled from the monument of Jesus. They bounced close together, like a cast of hundreds of tiny blue dancers waltzing to Bach's "Minuet in G", heavenly music played by an orchestra of angelic musicians. The bubbles dipped down beckoning to Sarah and Charlie, and began to swirl faster as they escorted the two new angels upward.

"In *Keeper of the Lambs*, the bubbles were the souls of unborn babies, aborted fetuses," I told them.

Denise listened attentively but with a look of dismay on her face.

"But how did you get that story about Sara's bubbles?"

"I wrote this four years ago, way before I met Sara," I explained. "These are excerpts from *Keeper of the Lambs*, one of my books, this one published in 2012."

"That is unbelievable!" Sara said looking at her parents who were taken aback.

"It's a sign!" I assured them. "The WAY has indeed led me to you, Sara, but just in case you need more proof, here is the dedication:

"To Lambs and blue bubbles, and to Sarah."

Chapter Four

Visions of An Elementary Student

By the time Sara was twelve years old, there was no denying she was different. Many of her experiences were of a serious nature, giving rise to the little girl's fears and worries about herself. But some of her experiences were light and funny. The best example of this was a crazy toy ambulance that went berserk in the living room of the Buccaneer. Denise was in another room, and Sara felt uncomfortable for some unexplainable reason. She watched a toy ambulance across the room from her, and the ambulance began making its siren sound even though no one had touched it.

"Mama, this ambulance is going off by itself!" Sara yelled and moved farther away from it. Denise came into the room and told Sara it probably just got bumped or something. Sara assured her no one had been near it. Suddenly, the ambulance started up, raced across the floor, and collided with Sara's foot. Sara pulled her feet up on the couch and screamed.

"Oh, Sara, stop that screaming! I'm sure it's just faulty batteries. Let me see it." Denise picked up the toy vehicle, popped open battery compartment and stared in disbelief. The compartment was empty—no batteries.

"Oh, it's just a stupid toy!" Denise put the toy away after giving a non-explanation but knew this was extremely unusual. She filed it away in the secret chamber of her brain becoming overloaded with unique Sara experiences.

Soon after the ambulance chasing, Sara had one of her most

memorable visions, one her mother could not dismiss.

"I saw a little girl about ten years old, carrying a doll and lingering in the hall outside my door." Sara told me in our first interview. "The little girl followed me, sometimes walking behind me and sometimes just watching me. She would come to my door, stop, and stare at me, and then turn around and walk up and down the hall again. I was completely freaked out. The girl looked at me with a blank stare, giving little or no facial expression, and she always had that doll with her. This went on for two weeks, and I couldn't go in the hallway at night."

The glassy-eyed stare of the little girl haunted Sara, more than usual, and she began shutting her door in an attempt to close out the little girl. Sara also started sleeping in complete darkness just so she wouldn't wake up and see the girl looking at her with her blank expression.

"We knew something was wrong." Randy added to the conversation, casting looks at the daughter he adored. "Sara always slept with her door open and had to have the light from the hall shining into her bedroom."

"When Sara told me what she was seeing, I tried to comfort her, but I truly did not understand, and to be truthful, most times I didn't believe in these ghosts who showed themselves only to my daughter." Denise admitted. "I prayed about it, and we prayed with Sara as a family."

Denise and her parents had always been a close family unit, and it was not uncommon for Denise to take out the box of old family photographs and go through them, reliving the memories of each family member and the occasion captured for posterity. Sara often sat with her mother enjoying the stories in the box. On this day, one special picture caught Sara's eye causing an excited reaction.

"We were just sitting there, Sara and me, looking at pictures, and all of sudden, she yelled and pointed to a picture in the box." Denise raised her voice to show how excited Sara became. "'That's her! That's the little girl who walks the hall and comes in my room!' Sara took the picture and held it close to her eyes. 'It's really her, Mama!'"

Denise smiled as her mind wandered back in time to a day many years before Sara's birth.

"This little girl was my friend's daughter. A bunch of us close friends were drawing names for Christmas presents one year, and I drew this little girl's name. Somehow she seemed to know because she came up to me and said, 'I'd like a Barbie doll for Christmas.' I just laughed and teased her saying, 'Go on, girl! I didn't get your name.'"

Denise's demeanor became serious as she told of the tragedy that followed a few days after drawing the little girl's name.

"I wish I could remember her name, but it was so long ago and my friend moved away shortly after. This sweet little girl had gone to check the mail and was coming back across the road to give the letters to her mom who watched from the porch. That was when it happened. A drunk driver going way too fast came around the curve and hit the girl, an enormous impact, propelling her into the air. People said this little one was thrown as high as a light pole that stood nearby and died on impact.

"It upset me when I heard of the little girl's death. All I could see was that sweet little grin as she told me she wanted a Barbie doll." Denise hugged Sara's daughter LeighAnna who was sitting beside her on the couch. "I bought a Barbie doll and put it in the casket with her so she would have the gift she had requested."

The doll carried by the spirit child was, in fact, a Barbie doll, and after this day, the little girl stopped showing herself to Sara. Perhaps it was the girl's way of saying thank you to Denise for giving her the Barbie, her constant companion.

As Sara grew older, her visions strengthened and began occurring more often. One day when Sara was in fifth grade, she noticed a tall, dark man dressed in a long black cape, standing outside the schoolyard fence close to the cafeteria canopy where she and her classmates always stood. One of the classmates standing with her was the new kid Nathan, a little boy taunted and picked on by the other students. Being tenderhearted, Sara befriended Nathan, and the two became best friends. Sara always gave her new friend her money for the canteen where he could buy snacks during recess; this was her way of showing Nathan he was her special friend.

The man stared at Sara, and she quickly turned away. No one seemed to notice him but her so she didn't say anything, not even to Nathan. By this time, she knew most of these images were seen by her alone, and she was careful not to blurt out when she saw a strange figure. For the next few days, the dark figure stood in the same spot, still staring at her. One day when she got home from school, she told her mother about the stranger. Denise was both frightened and angry and rode by the school several times the next day hoping to catch the man as he stared at her little girl. But Denise never saw the man, and neither did Sara see him anymore at school.

By the end of the week, Nathan had moved, and Sara lost her new friend. Soon after this, Sara's parents read in the newspaper where Nathan and his sister had been killed in a car accident.

Later, Sara identified the man in the black cape as a Grim Reaper of sorts, but without the rickety coach and horses and without the skeletal features associated with Death Incarnate. This man would become the vision she feared most.

"Today, if I see this man with the black cape, it freaks me out. Ninety percent of the time when I see this dark shadow with a black cape, someone I know will die." Sara's eyes showed the uneasiness she feels thinking and talking about the possibility of seeing the caped man.

Will the death be an acquaintance, a well-known member of her community, a distant family member, or will it be someone special, someone close? These questions haunt Sara each time she sees the man in the black cape.

Chapter Five

Uncle Johnny

Sara's teen years brought stronger, more consistent encounters with the paranormal and more denial from both herself and her family. This beautiful blonde teenage girl, a cheerleader with a normal outward demeanor, could not possibly be this different. But prayers continued unabated as Sara recalled each unique experience to her parents, experiences she was forced to endure without real understanding. Her family remained in a state of silence, especially outside the family home, but the silence could not halt Sara's unique events from gaining strength as she matured.

"When I was a teenager, I walked into the living room one December morning, and as I rounded the corner by the Christmas tree, I jumped, startled by what I saw! A nice looking man dressed in a leather jacket stood looking at the tree. When I jumped, he saw me and jumped, just as alarmed as I was, and then he disappeared right before my eyes.

"He didn't look like someone from nowadays with his dark slicked back hair, but he was very handsome. I had never seen him before." Sara smiled remembering the nice looking man, a possible lookalike of James Dean, the famous actor who died in a car wreck when only twenty-five years of age.

"A while later, when I was at my grandmother's, she had a picture out of her brother Johnny who died before I was born. He would have been my great Uncle Johnny. When I saw it, I yelled, 'That's him! That's the man I saw at the Christmas tree!'"

At this point, my heart began palpitating as I remembered another character from *Keeper of the Lambs*.

"Black leather jacket? I bet he rode a motorcycle, didn't he?" I looked at Sara and her parents, but already knew what the answer was before they shook their heads confirming this. "Oh, my! Don't tell me he was murdered?" I noticed my audience looked bewildered.

"Yes, he was. How did you know?" Randy asked, eager to hear my answer.

"*Keeper of the Lambs*—and I bet his body was not discovered until some time later—probably outdoors how he liked to spend his time." My response drew more looks, but we got sidetracked after Randy and Denise told me they really didn't know many details other than he was murdered.

Sara found out more information about Uncle Johnny a few days later at my request. Johnny was a young man, very handsome, often rode a motorcycle, and was murdered but his murder remains unsolved. His body was found outdoors, away from where he was murdered since autopsy evidence indicated his body had been moved, and it was found a good while after he disappeared.

The next visit I had with Sara, she told me her dad was leaving for work and wanted to know how he could get a copy of *Keeper of the Lambs* since it was an eBook, and he had no way to read it electronically. I went upstairs and found a copy I had printed out for entry in a contest. I signed the manuscript and sent it to him with the following direction: "Tell Randy to pay close attention to Johnny as he reads."

Idaho
The Present
After a few jarring minutes, the vehicle stopped. The driver exited and opened the door behind his seat putting Billie on high alert. The groans and heavy breathing of the man fueled more fear in her as he pulled and lifted something heavy from the back. The scent of Johnny permeated her surroundings heightening her sense of smell. But his cologne was overpowered by a different smell.

"Metal or iron, maybe." (she thought).

The smell wafted through the air and into her nostrils; it was a strong smell that found its way into the back of her mouth, giving her a taste she did not want to experience.

"Blood!"

...New tears soaked the blindfold, and low whimpering sounded from the back of the vehicle as the girl realized the nightmare was just beginning.

Johnny would not rescue her.

Billie could only pray that death would not follow her and the small life forming in her body, all that was left of Johnny, the life Johnny had demanded they end. She closed her eyes as the drug and terror induced drowsiness took control.

...

The boot looked like a man's black lace-up boot, the kind a motorcyclist would wear, but (Zach) had to look farther and make sure there was not a female body in the area...There was no way he could determine when the person was killed. The body was not decomposed that much, but it could have been buried and then dragged from its burial site recently. Zach needed to know if another body had been buried with the motorcyclist.

(Excerpt from Keeper of the Lambs by Dr. Sue Clifton, MuseItUp Publishing, 2012)

After Randy had begun to read *Keeper of the Lambs,* he sent me a message by Sara.

"Tell Sue, Johnny had a brother named Billy."

Chapter Six

"Stuff like that..."

The older and more mature Sara became, the more her experiences intensified. The appearance of her great Uncle Johnny was the first of many visions in her teenage years, years plagued with personal torment as Sara continued to view being different with increased disdain and fear, especially when her experiences seemed to predict changes in the family members she loved.

One member of Sara's family had a harder time dealing with Sara's difference than the rest of the family and openly expressed it once yelling to Sara "You're just crazy!" Sara had just had a frightening experience and reacted to it.

"I was in Mama's room and I heard something. I said 'Who's there?' I got an answer; a deep male voice said, 'It's me.' I took off running out of the room and felt like somebody was right behind me. I hyperventilated showing my parents just how frightened I was and they tried to calm me down. This is when my cousin who was staying with us yelled, 'You're just crazy!' I got fighting mad and screamed back at her, 'I'm not crazy! I'm not crazy!'

"I'm shaking; my face is blood red, and my parents are holding me back trying to calm me when all I want to do is get hold of my cousin. Mama yells, 'Baby, stop! Calm down!' But I've totally lost it."

The more energy Sara exerted in her own frenzied defense, the more things began to happen. The ceiling fan, which was turned off at the time, began slowly turning its blades, building its momentum with each revolution, the blades going faster, faster, faster! In seconds the fan was rotating out of control and gyrating as if it were going to fly off the ceiling.

"I'm hysterical at this point and Daddy yelled to my cousin, 'Get out of here!' I held on to my cousin feeling like I could tear her apart I was so angry, and Daddy shoved the door with his foot, breaking my hold on her and the door banged shut. Daddy yelled for Mama to keep the bedroom door shut while he calmed me down. When I got control, the fan blades slowed and then stopped completely. 'This will never leave this room!' Daddy spoke in a serious, no nonsense voice, and we knew to mind him on this one."

"I don't know if it had anything to do with this or not, but Sara was real sick at the time." Denise added. "She was a high school cheerleader and was always busy with that, and she came down with severe anemia. She was real weak, didn't feel good most of the time, and we didn't know at the time how sick she was."

Sara's feelings of insecurity caused her parents anguish almost equal to their daughter's anxiety. Both parents toiled with helping their daughter gain confidence and comfort.

Besides feeling on edge at her parents' nice Buccaneer home, Sara also had a problem going to her mom's friend's house. As a teenager, Sara was often invited to spend the night out there, but her mom always went with her and even slept with Sara if she was too afraid or uneasy. During one of their visits with Denise and Sara sharing a bed like usual, Sara slept fine, but when they awoke the next morning, she and her mom were unnerved to find Sara's nightgown had been taken off during the night.

"I told Latrice, Mom's friend, I had no idea how my nightclothes were removed, but she did not believe me. She said I just got hot and took them off without waking up. I was never a heavy sleeper and knew this was not what happened but neither Mom nor I could explain it." Sara looked to her mom for confirmation.

"That was not the only time it happened." Denise took up the story. "A couple of times after that, Sara and I spent the night there and woke up to the same thing each morning. Sara's nightclothes had been taken off, and Sara did not remember doing it, did not know how it happened and neither did I. I think I would have woke up if Sara started peeling her clothes off. There was no logical explanation."

Again Sara tried to convince Latrice of her innocence in disrobing herself, but Latrice's skepticism was unyielding. But she had a plan for the next time Sara and Denise spent the night.

"I'll fix you this time, Miss Sara. There's no way you will get out of this gown!" The friend brought in an old fashioned long sleeved gown that fastened with buttons from the ankles all the way up the back, ending at the nape of her neck. Sara and her mother slept soundly that night, somewhat relieved to know Sara's gown would still be on when they woke up.

Sara awoke late the next morning and walked into the kitchen to join her mother and her friend who were already having coffee.

"My hair was standing out all over my head like I'd tossed and turned all night, and I had to hold it out of my face, but I didn't realize anything until my mother almost choked on a sip of coffee. She and Latrice stared at me with big eyes like they were in shock. The gown, the one impossible for me to get out of, was turned wrong side out and was on me backwards but with all the buttons still buttoned—all the way up to my chin."

Latrice could not explain this but, being very religious, she still refused to think it could be anything connected with the house she lived in—the house that always frightened her friend's daughter.

Sara's visions began taking on a protective role where her parents were concerned, especially after Sara married and moved from their home.

"If I saw one of my parents in a vision, it terrified me." Sara checked through her notebook to find one of the visions she had noted for our first interview.

"I learned it could be about something bad already passed or could possibly be a foreshadowing of something about to happen but I was unsure each time I had one. For instance, one day I was putting some clothes in the washer, and I looked around and saw my mama all dressed up with makeup on, but in reality, Mama was not dressed up at all and was getting ready for bed. A week later, Mama was in the hospital and could not even sit up without her blood pressure going dangerously high. She was dressed up just like in my vision when she got so sick and had to be taken to the hospital."

Another time while away, Sara called her parents' house and in an excited voice asked her mother, "What's wrong with Daddy's ankle? Why is he limping?"

"Nothing is wrong with Daddy, Sara; he's out in the yard." Denise answered, but as soon as she hung up, Randy came in the door limping and asked who was on the phone.

"It was Sara asking me what was wrong with your ankle." Denise watched as Randy sat down, took his shoe off, and began rubbing his ankle.

"Call her back and ask her which ankle?" Randy assured Denise he was serious.

"Your daddy wants to know which ankle?" Denise held the receiver away from her mouth to give Randy Sara's answer. "She said the left one." Denise and Randy laughed even though Randy continued to rub his ankle—his left ankle.

Sara could always sense when something was happening to one of her parents even if it was something trivial such as having an image of ice cubes falling while at the same exact moment her mother choked on a Freeze Pop. Or the time Sara had a vision of her parents on the road with yellow lights flashing all around them. Sara frantically called her mom and asked, "What are all those flashing lights?" The lights were yellow warning lights for the major construction in the road as Randy and Denise passed through the construction zone.

Some visions happened at critical times in Sara's parents' lives. Randy had been diagnosed with stage four cancer, and in one of his weakest moments, Denise had to take him to the hospital after hours. Randy, too weak to make it on his own but determined to try, managed to get trapped between two sets of glass doors going into the hospital much to Denise's alarm. By the time she rescued him from the doors, Sara was on the phone hysterical wanting to know, "Why is my daddy behind a glass door?"

Sara's visions and feelings continued into her marriage even though her husband was skeptical. The young couple rented a house, one Sara should have known better than to rent. Her sister had rented the same house years earlier, and while spending the night there, Sara had felt someone shake her and pull her hair. Regardless, the young family rented the same house only to have even more mysterious things happen this time. They would hear a rocking chair creaking as it rocked back and forth in a steady, ghostly rhythm, but when they looked, the chair stood motionless and silent. And practically every night people were heard walking up and down the hallway.

"The thing that unnerved me the most was something that happened to my daughter who was pre-school at the time. I'd hear LeighAnna talking and playing with someone, and I just shrugged it off as an imaginary friend. It really didn't alarm me since I had my blue bubbles as a child and never found them frightening.

"One day I heard her jumping on her bed, but it sounded like two sets of feet jumping with the second set hitting the bed a second or two after the first ones. I opened her bedroom door and asked her what she was doing. She told me, 'We're just jumping on the bed.' I let the 'we' go, but then I heard a thud and LeighAnna started crying. I opened the door and ran to LeighAnna as she sat on the floor. While I wiped away her tears, she looked up at me and said, 'He pushed me!' LeighAnna was never afraid of the dark, but after that day, she had to have a light on in the hall. This was not like my child. It all changed because of the imaginary friend, and I got worried this friend was not a good friend like my bubbles."

In addition to the imaginary friend and the footsteps, Sara's family would leave and when they would come home, cabinet doors would be open and the lights on, lights that had been turned off when they left. Having quite enough frightening experiences, Sara and her family soon moved out of the house. Another woman moved in right away, and a few weeks later, Sara saw the woman and was asked a question confirming the experiences of her own family.

"She asked me if we ever had strange things happen when we lived in the house and I told her we had. She told me she was in the shower one day, and the shower curtain pulled open by itself." Sara laughed as she told the next part. "She said she ran out of the house naked."

One of Sara's most frightening and mystifying experiences

happened when LeighAnna was just a baby. Sara was staying with her sister one night and she had a friend there also. When the friend got ready to go home at about ten or eleven o'clock, Sara offered to take her knowing LeighAnna would get sleepy while riding in her infant seat in the back.

"I had to drive the back roads to get to the girl's house, and on my way back after dropping her off, something big hit my windshield. It was huge and black like a bird but not like a normal bird. This is exactly what I saw. The thing had the neck and wings of a big bird but the head of a human baby. When it hit the windshield, it's cheek squished against the glass, and its eyes were white and looked straight at me. It cracked its neck around in jerky movements and flew off leaving drool all over the windshield. When I got to my parents' house, I was in shock, and my parents had to help me out of the car." Sara looked at her mother who took up the story from there.

"Wet, slimy stuff was smeared all over the windshield, and Sara was shaking when we got her and the baby out of the car. A couple of days later, I was talking to Mama's cousin who lived on those back roads, and I asked her if they ever saw anything scary down by the creek. That was where Sara had to go that night. The cousin told me, 'Mama taught us never to go to the creek 'cause bird people live there.'"

"I have gone on that road a few times since that night, but I've never seen the bird thing again." Sara finished the story with a shiver.

Nowhere was safe, and Sara was not immune to visions anywhere she went. Once while in church, she saw a man get up from his pew and leave his body. She told me how he moved right through people sitting nearby. He stopped and stared at his body sitting there on the bench. A few minutes later, she saw the man reenter his body. Within a week, the man had died.

Even though Sara's gift is predominantly communicating with or seeing those who have passed, on occasion, she is able to see future events—headline events, not that she can do anything to stop them. With Sara, she can be going about her daily duties or be somewhere just having fun when out of nowhere comes something similar to the old special broadcast announcement "We interrupt this program…" But one "interruption" to her normal thinking and doing process that stands out more than others was her seeing a gigantic ball of fire hitting the earth.

"One day, just out of the blue I had a vision of huge orange and white balls of fire shooting down from the sky at an angle. They were not coming straight down but at an angle like this." Sara dips her hand to show the slant of the ball descending. "These huge balls of fire propelled fast, and the earth was the target in one of the most frightening visions I have ever had. I could feel the ground rumbling and hear glass breaking with tremendous force. And the smells were overbearing: the dust from the ground as the huge balls of fire hit; metallic smells of buildings crashing; and the smoke and the fire emblazoned on the whole landscape giving off toxic fumes. I didn't just see it; I felt it through every one of my senses. But the worst sensation was hearing the screams of people caught in the showers sent from the fiery explosions in the air. Fire literally rained down on people below.

"I experienced this same vision for four days in a row and was totally unnerved by it. I'd walk outside and look up, wondering if this was going to happen here where my family was. I was exhausted with worry from feeling this was a premonition of something big that was going to happen and I could do nothing about it but pray.

"Frantic, I went to my Mom's and told her and my dad what I had seen in a vision, several visions really. I told them I felt like something was going to happen and I needed them to watch the news. I've never been one to watch the news with the gift I have, not wanting to know things that might be revealed to me later. Also I see so much more than what is on that TV screen with different images and people bombarding me with information and messages. It gives me anxiety attacks.

"I got a piece of paper and drew what I had seen—a ball of orange and white fire coming down with a trail like jet airplanes have, but this was a white fiery trail, not just a line. I told my parents it could be an airplane crashing to earth but it was so big! Daddy told me, 'It sounds like a meteor. I'll watch the news close and let you know if I see or hear anything reported.'"

"I was so scared for the earth!" Sara continued. "And then it happened. A week after I told my parents, Daddy called and said, 'Come over; I have to show you something.' When I got there, Daddy walked to the TV and pressed a button. 'Is this what you saw?' Daddy turned on the special news broadcast he had recorded. 'Holy crap! You described it to a T!' I sat and watched with my dad, exactly what I had seen the week before."

On February 15, 2013, a 10,000-ton meteor, 55 feet in diameter, lit up the sky over the Ural Mountains of Russia with the power of thirty times the energy of the atomic bomb dropped on Hiroshima. The meteor mostly disintegrated just above the earth but a total of 53 fragments hit the earth. The supersonic speed of the meteor caused explosions on the ground causing damage to 3000 buildings and injuring over a thousand people.

The films showing the meteor approaching the earth looked exactly as Sara had seen in her visions a week before it happened: "A ball of orange and white fire coming down with a trail like jet airplanes have, but this was a white fiery trail, not just a line."

Sara tries not to do readings on her family. She "closes herself off to them emotionally because it causes tremendous anxiety on her part, and she feels she is too attached. But as in the story of Great Uncle Johnny, sometimes they seek her as their personal emissary when they feel the need to bring peace to a beloved family member left behind.

This was the case with Sara's cousin James. Though they were kin, there was an age difference as well as a difference in living styles for Sara and her cousin, so she had never thought about James contacting her. Sara remembered well the terrible phone call she had received in 2008, on leap year, telling her James, her daddy's nephew, had committed suicide by shooting himself. Her grandmother Dulaney was distraught over losing her grandson and never really got over it. Perhaps, what bothered her most was the belief those who commit suicide are doomed to hell.

About three months ago, Sara began to "feel" James trying to communicate with her, and she tried to connect with him by looking at his picture. Immediately, she "got a few things such as the letter M, a name with a butterfly tattoo above it, and a few images here and there that, as most times, did not make sense to her. Sara felt compelled to call her Grandmother and when she got her on the phone, she asked to be put on speakerphone. This was so she could speak to James' mother Janice and her grandmother at the same time.

"I told my grandmother and aunt that James was with me. It's hard to explain but I could feel his presence. James kept talking about crazy stuff I hoped made sense to my grandmother and aunt."

From the first when Sara realized she was different, her grandmother Dulaney and that side of the family had accepted it and did not judge her. Sara was comforted by not having to hide her experiences from these family members.

"James told me his chest hair is just in patches spotted around his chest." Sara told them, and Janice validated this and said it was weird how it grew. "He talked about holding his tongue after he had it pierced and said he couldn't talk when it got infected and was too swollen." Again Janice confirmed what Sara told them.

"I think he told me all of this just so his mom and our grandmother would know it was really him talking to me." Sara explained how many times those who contact her use trivial information for her to give their loved ones, something for them to validate it is really they talking through her.

"Once that credibility is established, it is much easier for the family member to accept the message," Sara explained. "James mentioned a big green ugly fish, his favorite belt buckle that his brother now wears, and little things like that. But then James got down to the real message he wanted to send his mother and grandmother.

"He didn't do it. James did not kill himself. He says J did it." Sara explained how many times she gets an initial rather than a full name. "He is letting you know he did not kill himself and wants to put your minds at ease about that. I picked up an M, and I saw him leaned over signing his name like signing a check. He wants M to know he thanks him for what he did."

Sara found out the M was for Mack, a friend of her Papaw Dulaney. Mack thought dearly of James and had paid for his funeral. James wanted Mack to know how much he appreciated it.

"Also, he did not have a major drug problem like some people said." Sara continued with the message. "He said, 'No, I was not on heavy drugs!' James threw his wallet with a chain attached down after saying this. He was so upset people thought he was a heavy drug user. He needed Grandmother Dulaney to know he was not on drugs and he did not kill himself.

"My grandma said if she died today, she was at peace. She always worried, thinking James would go to hell for taking his own life. This was what she had been taught in church. A lot of people think someone who commits suicide is doomed to hell and can't receive forgiveness."

Another thing James showed her was a name with a butterfly tattoo over it. When Sara told this, Janice confirmed she had a tattoo with James' name and a butterfly over it, something she did after losing her son.

"James is with his cousin Jeremy, Bobby's son," Sara added. Jeremy was another Dulaney tragedy having died in a car accident. Jeremy had lived with Randy and Denise after Bobby's death, and they were very attached to him. Sara went on to tell about another paranormal happening connected with Jeremy.

"One day Jeremy and my mom were walking together and Jeremy stepped over a penny. Mom told him, 'You need to stop and pick that up, Jeremy. Don't you know when you see a penny, it's a loved one sending you a message from heaven?'" Sara smiled as she told this story, one of her Mom's favorites.

"Mom made Jeremy pick that penny up, and it became a standing joke between them. Neither of them ever passed up a penny again."

On the day of Jeremy's funeral, Denise was in the shower sobbing over losing Jeremy. She felt something hit her on the top of the head, and when she looked down, there lay a shiny penny on the floor of the shower.

"Well, I guess you're okay, Jeremy!" Denise laughed as she

picked up the penny.

A friend of mine named Hilda was with Sara and me on one of our most productive and mystifying excursions. Hilda had already been "read" by Sara before the two met, but that story will come in a later chapter. On the trip, Hilda asked Sara if anyone, perhaps in other generations in her family, had ever experienced the same gift.

Sara answered with, "Somewhere way back, a woman in our family was born with a veil over her face. Nobody ever talked about it though. I didn't have a veil, but I was supposed to die before I was born. Maybe that's the reason I was born different. I'm pretty sure my son has my gift and my daughter has seen some things, too."

Sara then began telling us about her children, Randyn three and LeighAnna nine, with her perceptions about their having the gift.

"One day, I was in a discount store, and Randyn was in the child seat of my cart when I saw an old man smoking a cigar. I told Randyn, 'That man is going to get in trouble smoking in here.' Randyn kept pointing at him, so I knew he saw him, too. I moved away from the man's stinky cigar smoke and headed for checkout. The cashier was talking to the woman in front of me and telling her how sorry she was for something that had happened. The customer answered by saying, 'Yes, I'm sorry, too, but he's in a better place now. People tell me they always knew when Daddy was around because of all that cigar smoke around him.'"

"Just stuff like that happens…" Sara said ending the disclosure as if this was an everyday occurrence for all people.

The "stuff" was never more evident than what happened when Randyn was just a baby.

"We were living in a camper by Mama and Daddy's house while our house was being built, and Randyn was just a toddler. Daddy had just been diagnosed with cancer, and I was glad I was near him and Mama. It was at this time, I started seeing a man I didn't know. The first time I saw him, he was propped against a tree. He pulled something out of his pocket that looked like a gold chain and held it out for me to see. I went on toward the house, and a few minutes later, I thought I saw someone go in the shed by the house. I figured it might be this guy so I told Daddy. Daddy looked but no one was in the shed.

"I kept seeing this guy but was not always sure if it was in a dream or if it was a vision. One day when I saw him it was raining, and I remember asking him in my mind, 'Who are you, and why won't you leave me alone?' He didn't answer me, but I knew this one was not going anywhere.

"Soon after that, I was at Mama's and Daddy's, and I put Randyn in the playpen for a nap. Daddy had a pair of binoculars out, and Randyn kept pointing at them wanting to play with them. He wouldn't go to sleep for trying to get Daddy to give him those binoculars.

"Daddy was afraid Randyn would hurt himself with them so he took the binoculars and threw them up on top of a tall chifferobe in the room. I told him he'd never be able to get those down, and he just said, 'Out of sight, out of mind.'

"We closed the door thinking Randyn would go to sleep, but we started hearing him giggling and playing. We went to check on him, and he was sitting up in the playpen playing with the binoculars. We knew there was no way he could have gotten them down.

"Within a few days, I saw the man again in a vision, this time standing under a sign that read Pecan; it was like a road sign. Again, he showed me the chain rolled up in his hand. I described the man to my dad, and he called his mother and told her about the vision I kept seeing. Daddy's mother told him it could be his younger brother Bobby who was killed in an accident when he was just a young man before I was born. Daddy dug through his family pictures and found a picture of my Uncle Bobby.

"When Randyn saw the picture, he started babbling 'Bob Bob' and making a sound with his fingers on his lips like when people give butterfly kisses. When I told Mama about the man holding a gold chain in his hand, she told me she knew it was Bobby. He loved to borrow her gold chain when he went on dates, and she always let him. Bobby was killed in a car wreck—just down from Pecan, the same road sign from my dream. Mama told me she laid her gold chain around Bobby's neck when he was in his casket. She couldn't clasp it so just left it loose under his shirt collar. That's why he always had it in his hand. Daddy said he thought his little brother had come back to watch over him while he was sick with cancer."

Things continued to get crazy at Sara's parents' house even after they figured out who Bobby was—things such as flying objects seen around the house and in the yard. Denise was having some construction done on the house, so Randy set up game cameras in the yard, both to check on the construction project since he and Denise were not there most of the time, and to "get to the bottom" of the strange flying objects. At one point, Denise asked some of the construction crew if they ever saw anything outside. She got her answer from one of the cameras that night. In one shot, an object was caught in two different positions under the big tree at the edge of the yard. In both pictures, the image seems to have extensions from his shoulders. In picture 1, he is standing to the left of the tree. In picture 2, he appears to have wings outstretched, ready for takeoff. Could Uncle Bobby have come back to earth as an angel, perhaps to watch over brother Randy?

Picture caught of being, possibly with wings.

Picture 2 caught of being with wings spread as if flying away

Chapter Seven

"Devil Child"

What could it be like for a young girl to see dead people and sights unseen by those around her; to answer aloud questions heard only by her; to go to a friend's house, one where she has never been, and walk straight to the girl's room without directions while her friend watches in dismay; to have to run from every room, avoiding the "someone" who seems to always be following?

From the time she was a toddler to her entry into adolescence, Sara learned she was different from other children. The more she asked her young friends, "Did you see that?" The more Sara discovered she was the only one witnessing the event; the more she tried to understand who or what she was, the more she felt alone, her negative thoughts drowning her in a sea of fear.

"I cried a lot as a child and I'd ask, 'Mama, why am I different?" Sara looked toward her mother who shook her head in agreement as she, too, remembered her daughter's fears and lack of comprehension of what was happening to her. But her mother was able to answer Sara's question and comfort her daughter in the only way she knew how—with arms and heart wide open.

From generations back, Sara's family identified themselves as devout, old fashioned, God-fearing Christians, the type who read their Bibles daily, pray or talk to God constantly, and feel ghosts and modern day visions and prophesies are evil and something to be avoided—or at least not spoken of publicly. Anything paranormal was contrary to Biblical teachings and was of the Devil Satan.

As Sara grew older, her mom was reminded many times of

Sara's episode with the "stinky poo poo man" in the haunted house and with her reaction when just three years old to the woman, a complete stranger, in the grocery store. With evidence of Sara's uniqueness growing as Sara herself grew to maturity, her own parents began to seek advice from older family members only to sometimes receive the warning "not to talk of such things which might be considered evil by others." And when Sara would try to talk to her parents about her "difference", their advice was always the same. "Let's keep it within the family boundaries and pray about it."

And pray Sara did, often, and fervently, many times with her head completely submerged under her bed covers to block out the sight of the phantom strangers trespassing in her room, appearing and then disappearing right before her eyes. With her bedroom door always open, and the hall light on, it was easy to see the figures coming and going but the door remained open. Sara was afraid of the dark and needed the comfort of thinking her parents could hear her if she screamed even though they were at the opposite end of the long house.

As Sara reached adolescence, her denial of her difference was no longer valid and no longer could be debunked or explained away as "too much imagination." Sara thought of herself as a devil child, not the "special angel" born from a strong mother's protective nature and selfless devotion to her unborn, at-risk baby. Sara feared being ostracized by friends and maybe even her family.

Praying! Begging God for understanding! Pleading with God to show mercy and take this burden from her and make her like other girls her age! Searching through the Bible for any passage that could explain who she was! Searching her own soul trying to find any goodness, any silver coating to combat the evil that dominated this "Devil Child!" These attempts at normality consumed this young girl.

The more Sara tried to overpower the dark by bringing in the light, the stronger her differences developed. "God, why am I different?" She cried one night until exhaustion overcame her and she fell asleep. And in the light cast across her bed from the hallway, Jesus sat on the bed beside her, smoothed her hair still wet from her tears, and mind to mind promised her rainbows; kittens and puppies without hope made well by her caring hands; children of her own who would love her unconditionally; parents who would not only some day understand her but who would support her in her quest to give comfort and peace to those in need; and the assurance that she is now and always will be a "God Child", a special angel sent to earth for a purpose to be revealed when she was mature enough to handle the responsibilities attached.

Sara prayed, went to church, read her Bible and wished for her difference to vanish as quickly as the visions had come, but The One In Control had other ideas. As the visions became more vivid, her denial became stronger. Even as a teenager and a young adult in her twenties, Sara only told her family and a couple of very close friends about these undesirable, unbelievable gifts. Engrained in her mind were the verses from the Bible *(translations other than KJV)*, the Old Testament mostly, warning against sorcerers, charmers, those who practice divination, and mediums or necromancers (those who speak to the dead). She did not want to be "an abomination unto the Lord", not to her Lord whom she had worshipped in church and learned about in Sunday school all her life.

At twenty-eight years of age, Sara, a mature married woman and the mother of two small children, was blessed with two visions that would change her life and make her accept her gift, realizing once and for all who she was.

In the first vision, Sara was going with her sister Brandy on a paranormal investigation, Sara's first, and even though she was not totally comfortable with the idea, she went because her sister wanted her to go. They stopped by the house of Jane, her sister's friend, and while Sara waited in the yard, she saw an elderly lady standing there.

"Who's the grandmother?" Sara asked as her sister exited the house.

"That's Jane's mother." Brandy answered as she got in the car and pulled away.

"No—the dead one?" Sara shocked her sister with the additional description even though her sister had always known about Sara's eccentricities.

"Uh ... I don't know. I think Jane's mother took care of her own mother before she died. I'll call Jane and ask her." Brandy took out her cell phone and called her friend. Just as she thought, the grandmother had died five years earlier and had been taken care of by Jane's mother.

"Jane's mother needs to know the most important question she has about her mother has been answered." Sara did not hesitate as she delivered the message she had received. "Please tell Jane her mother's hump is gone from her back; she can stand as straight as a board; and she can even lean over and garden. She is pain free and very happy. She knew her daughter was still worrying about this and needed to know."

Brandy relayed the message to Jane who called Sara a few minutes later and told her how her mother had cried tears of happiness when she heard her own mother's message. This was the answer to the one question Jane's mother had wanted answered above all others. She had not been able to let her mother go but now she could.

Jane's mother called a few minutes later and said something that night that started the change in Sara's attitude toward her supernatural talent.

"You have helped me so much. To know my mother is no longer in pain and can stand straight is the most wonderful gift anyone could give me. Thank you, Sara."

"I had given that lady comfort, and in her thank you, she had given me the comfort I needed to declare to the world and to myself, I have a gift, a gift from God, and I need to use it in good faith to bring peace and closure to those in need."

The second event finalized the positive change brewing in Sara's thinking.

Sara's Grandpa Dulaney was in the hospital not expected to live. Not only was Sara worried about her grandfather, she was also worried about her own dad and how this loss would affect him. In Randy's words, here is what happened:

"Thinking I would lose my dad was really hard on me. My Dad and I were always real close. When Sara arrived at the hospital, she tried to talk to him, but he just seemed to have a distant look on his face. Sara thought he looked scared, but then she said she could see calm in his eyes. She asked him if he could see them. He didn't answer her but she said she could see the relief in his eyes; she was seeing what he did.

"Sara and me walked out of the room, and she told me he was seeing his mother and his son. They passed before Sara was born. She told me they were waiting on him. The next day or so my dad kept saying he would 'be glad when that car gets here.' I thought he was talking about one of us so we could bring him home. After about three or four times of saying it, my mom asked him, 'What kind of car are you waiting on?' He told her, 'A Model T Ford—Momma and Bobby are coming to get me.' Mom's mouth dropped open.

"Just knowing your loved one has those who love him with all their heart, standing by to be with them when they leave you—it just makes it easier to accept."

"The devil don't like peace and happiness," Sara told me smiling. "And the devil does not do good." Sara had seen those from her grandfather's life waiting for him and he did, too. After seeing them there in the hospital room and telling her dad about it, she could see the peace it brought him, and it made her see how important her gift was. Even though God changed his mind and didn't take her grandfather at that time, Sara knows her dad can handle it when the day does come.

"That's when I knew for sure I was not a devil child. I have a gift; I have a purpose, and if I stay open to it, I can help people just like I helped my dad."

Soon after this, Sara started her Angel Leigh Facebook Page where she does readings for people who contact her. Leigh is Sara's middle name, and as Sara explained the other part, "I often see angels rather than spirits in my visions." And Denise had called her daughter "my special angel" before she was born. Perhaps visions run in Sara's family!

A few months later, when I met Sara for the first time, I did not meet a shy young woman who was apologetic for being able to communicate with dead people. I met a young woman quick to tell me she was a Christian, entrusted with a special gift given to her by God.

By the end of the shoot for the TV show, I had seen this gift in action many times; I had smiled with those receiving their messages from a mom and a favorite grandmother, and I had shed tears knowing my daughter-in-law had been blessed by Sara's gift with a message from a mother who had passed three years prior but who would never pass from her daughter's heart.

Writing Sara's book was a given after that first meeting, and Sara and I have become close friends. But it was on one of our other trips to a very old, historical cemetery that Sara gave a very impromptu, heartwarming explanation of her gift, letting me know in no uncertain terms who she is.

I always carry my camcorder when I am with Sara, not wanting to miss any information and personal stories she might decide to share with me. I wanted to see and write Sara's life through her eyes and her voice, and I wanted to make sure I didn't miss anything important. As we walked along that day looking for information on a little lost boy Sara had seen on her first trip to the cemetery, Sara reached down and picked a tiny yellow flower. With the little flower held securely in her fingertips, Sara began her narrative.

"I had a vision one time that included a yellow flower." Sara held her hand out showing me the tiny flower now placed in her palm. "We were in an old two story building with all kinds of old metal chairs, tables, and equipment, maybe like an operating room or a hospital. People were following me, and all of a sudden a huge dark mist came upon us! The others were terrified, and I looked back and told them, 'Don't be afraid; you are protected and you are going to see through my eyes.'

"We all held hands, and a blue and white light surrounded me and then spread around each person in the group. The wind was blowing hard and sounded like a train, the ground rumbled, and the dark mist collided with me, but I was still not afraid. I looked down and the floor cracked open, and as it did, big angel wings came up behind me. Knowing I had an angel with me, I was not afraid, and instead of running away from the dark mist, I moved toward it still holding hands with the people behind me. The light grew brighter, and the angel sent the demon into the crack and sealed the ground over him.

"Through my eyes, everyone saw the lost souls who had been held captive. An old woman and a little girl walked up to me before heading toward the light awaiting them, and the woman smiled as she put her hand on the little girl's shoulder. I bent down on one knee and smiled up into the little girl's face, and she held out a tiny yellow flower to me just like this."

Sara showed me the flower again and then closed her hand as she continued.

"I folded my hand with the flower inside and it was like I woke up then. But it wasn't a dream; it was a vision. I put my hand to my face and felt my nose bleeding, and when I opened my hand, there was this little yellow flower."

Sara opened her hand back up at this moment and held the little yellow flower out to me. Even though this was a reenactment, I had a comforting sensation to wash over me. Sara began interpreting the vision for me.

"I knew then I was here for only good—God gave me this gift. The lost souls who were held captive went to the light. God let me help save them. I'm not a medium. That's a bad thing in the Bible. I don't do demon stuff or witchcraft. I'm here to help people with their grief. I don't seek the dead; they seek me and give me messages to take back to their loved ones who can't stop grieving. I'm a Messenger for God's people who have passed. So far everything I've done has been for the good. When I'm in places like this cemetery, or in houses or buildings that are supposed to be haunted, I can run into negative forces. That is why I pray before I ever go in and I pray again at the end and thank God for the protection.

"I'm not here to prove myself to anyone. I grew up full-blown Christian; I'm tenderhearted, and I pray about everything. On my first investigation with Mississippi Paranormal Investigations, I got a little girl's name and no one had been able to get it before. A lot of times, I connect with the ones who have not been noticed. Even if it's just a 'Hey, I've got the dog with me,' that right there means something to someone.

"I run into negativity a lot, but it's not my job to send that demon back to hell." *Sara covers her mouth with her hand in apology.* "Excuse my language but I'm not here for that. I'm here for those who need to get a message out. A simple 'I'm okay' means a lot to those loved ones.

"This is who I am. I do everything through faith—no cards or Ouija boards. I don't fault those who use other means; that's not my place but this is how I do it. I prayed for God to lead the way even before I did the Angel Leigh page, and I let him lead me in everything I do. For years I struggled and asked Him, 'What am I?' There are others like me and I know they're struggling, too. I pray to get the messages that need to be delivered. I know now I am a Messenger who brings peace and closure.

"People can say I'm a fake or a devil person, but God knows my heart. If I can help someone through the storm, even just one person, then I've done what God wants me to do."

Sara nods her head signifying she's through with her interpretation and heads off to another section of the cemetery.

In that old, neglected cemetery that day, Sara, in her own words and without knowing it, had just been a Messenger for me. As the author of Sara's book, I, too, was struggling. The more I searched the Bible for scriptures to support my friend and her gift, the more I found verses in the Old Testament condemning mediums, categorizing it with sorcery and witchcraft. I was also seeking reassurance in the Bible and on the Internet for myself after reading all the verses warning against mediums and seeking the dead. I needed something that would show me what I'm writing about is okay with my Heavenly Father.

And there it was—an article that stated the term "medium" is never used in the New Testament. In fact, the term does not exist in the Old Testament or New Testament in the King James Version. Even the terms necromancers and familiar spirits, as in "consulting with familiar spirits", are not found in the King James Version of the

Bible. I know the Old Testament is the Word of God and is a history of His people, but I also know my salvation comes about because of the birth of Jesus Christ. I read the Bible, New Testament more than the Old, and I pray, but I have been remiss in the last six months on both, not doing either like I have most of my life. But in that old cemetery, the ultimate truth was laid before me in the most eloquent, yet down to earth oratory I've ever been privileged to hear. I was reassured what I'm writing and what Sara is doing are God sent. This marvelous young woman let me see her life, her faith, her beliefs, and her works *Through the Eyes of Angel Leigh.*

Sara is not a Medium. Sara is a Messenger!

(3 John 1:11) …Anyone who does what is good is from God. Anyone who does what is evil has not seen God.

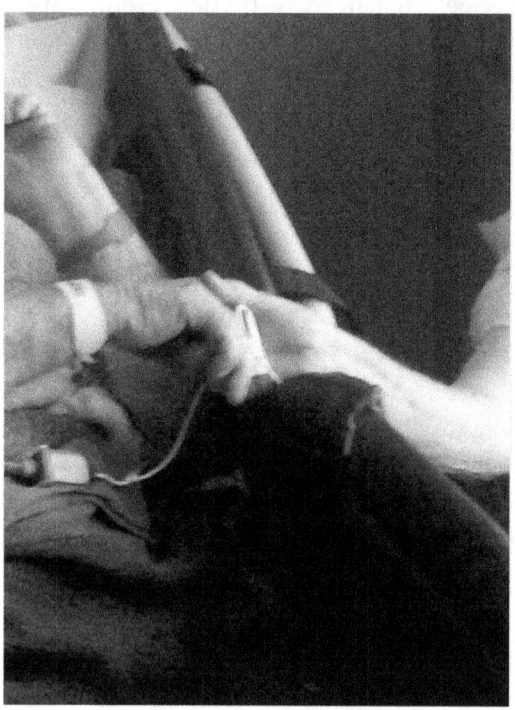

Grandparents Dulaney holding hands in the hospital

Part II

Angel Leigh

Chapter Eight

Messages

Who is Angel Leigh?

Angel Leigh is the same tenderhearted, young Christian woman known as Sara Dulaney Pugh. Five months ago, Sara accepted her gift, took a leap of faith, and opened herself up to be a messenger for those who have passed. Her Angel Leigh Facebook page is where she does readings for people still grieving from the loss of a loved one.

Grief is devastating, and we all grieve in our own ways. Not everyone seeks messages from those passed, but for those of us who want the comfort of a message, Sara makes herself available. As a Christian, Sara believes it is her calling, a gift from God backed by real understanding, maturity, strength, and acceptance of the responsibilities attached, all in the name of "providing peace and comfort to those who need closure." It took almost twenty-nine years, her lifetime, for Sara to accept the responsibility attached to her gift, but now she embraces it and the role she is to play with her whole heart and being, always backed by prayer.

"The one thing I want each person to remember when requesting a reading from me is I am not a medium; I am a messenger." Sara is adamant in expressing there is a difference.

"I do not seek the dead; the dead seek me, most of the time after a person grieving has reached out and requested my help and opened themselves up to receiving messages, but sometimes these messages are spontaneous, unrequested. I don't give advice but I do offer comfort; I don't predict the future; I am a messenger only." Being a Christian and very tenderhearted, Sara does admit to having emotional attachment to her clients and often keeps in contact with them. She even has whole families as clients.

How does it all work? Is the deceased following the living around, watching them cry, worry, wring their hands, or sit at home in hopeless despair? Possibly—but not even Sara knows how or why she receives these messages. A client can begin the process by giving Sara a name or a picture of a loved one and the rest is up to the deceased. Sara asks for no additional information, and in fact, has had to turn down persons asking for readings because they gave too much information too early. Nor does she seek information from the internet, newspapers, or any usual source. Sara insists "Information must come from the deceased." As messages begin coming to her, Sara writes everything down in a notebook even if it makes no sense at all to her.

"Ditto!"

Everyone remembers the movie *Ghost*—how could anyone forget Patrick Swayze, Demi Moore, and of course, the remarkable and funny "medium" Oda Mae Brown played by Whoopi Goldberg. Oda Mae, when finally realizing what she is, has to convince Molly that Sam is really sending her messages from the afterlife through her, Oda Mae, and the magic word "ditto" is the trigger to make Molly a believer. True, this wonderful movie is fiction but could it happen?

How can someone seek and receive messages from a loved one now deceased? Where does this process begin?

"Validation is most important for the messenger and for the recipient," explains Sara. "If someone requests a reading from me, it is my job to establish credibility first, but the only way this can be done is through giving information known only by the client and the deceased—trivia, if you will. One phrase Sara hears almost as much as "thank you" is the term "spot on" as in "You were spot on in what you told me about _____."

"Every word is important, has meaning to someone." Sara never takes any message lightly. Even "ditto" can mean something special to the right person.

And what is the one question every client wants answered above all others? "Is he or she okay?" Interpreted, this could mean "Tell me you're not in pain!" or "Tell me you still love me!" or "Tell me you're not in hell!" Only the client and the deceased know what meaning fits.

This book would not be Sara's story without showing how she has helped her clients to deal with their loss or losses. Part II, Angel Leigh, is a collection of the readings Sara has done in the five months she has been Angel Leigh. Confidentiality is key to Sara, and absolutely no information is included unless the client has given permission for text and/or pictures to be used. In many of the readings, names and places have been changed to protect the privacy of the individuals even though they want their story told. Much of the stories are told in narrative, but many are actual dialogue from the readings. Many times, the quickly scribbled notes of Angel Leigh will be shown, her "validation that messages are real." Other notes will be shown in the appendices with a brief synopsis.

And how does Sara receive these messages? Does she go into a trance? Do her eyes roll back in her head? I can answer this question after seeing and filming her in action on many occasions. She goes very still except for her fingertips which are working overtime, sort of leans her head to one side, and the pupil in one eye gets larger. She knows where she is, but her present surroundings often become distorted as new people and places come forward. On one occasion when she was seeing a spirit of a female in a white dress, the woman was reflected in the pupil of her dominant eye and caught on camera. *(This is the picture used for the cover; it a profile in the gray part next to her pupil on the right side).* Unless you know Sara, you would not be able to tell when she is receiving a message—that is until she grabs a pen and starts jotting down words and phrases in the notebook she always keeps handy.

Sara explains her experience this way:

"I experience spirits in many different ways. I can see and hear them, and at times, I can pick up emotions. It all comes to me like moving pictures. I sometimes will get images that are blurry, but in the end, it all makes sense. I've done this since I was about three years old. It is something I've always had, but I only recently started using my gift purposely to help people."

Can we be with our loved ones and family members who passed before us? Is it possible to have a second chance to be with Jesus? Will we get to be with our beloved pets? Will we be able to see what's going on with families and friends still living? Read each example of Sara's readings, and you will find possible answers to these questions.

Now get out the tissues, put your feet up, and open your heart to "messages from beyond" relayed to loved ones through Angel Leigh.

Chapter Nine

Cheyenne and Dakota

Not long ago, Sara was browsing on a general medium site when her eyes stopped on the wedding picture of a beautiful young couple. Sara grabbed her notebook and began scribbling words and phrases, not taking time to use lines or neatness, as the messages began pouring into her mind. Sara immediately contacted the girl whose name was Cheyenne.

"Hey! I was drawn to you tonight and feel I can help you."

When the girl expressed interest, Sara dove right in, looking at her notes and talking about everything she could see in her mind. She knows the soul sending the message is establishing credibility so Cheyenne will know it is he talking through her, his messenger.

"Did he like pizza? I smell pizza." Sara begins and then changes the subject. "He told me about the pole incident. He knows someone took down the stuff and a lot of people came together, stood together to get it all back on the pole. He talks of a girl, initial B and someone named Ed or Edward. Your husband loves you and misses you and is sorry he had to go so soon. He shows me blue balloons floating in the sky and says, 'Yep! That was for me!' He knows how much you mourn him, and yes, you can do this because he knows how strong you are. 'Quit blaming God!' This is what he stresses and says he knows it's not fair, but it was his time to go. Dakota hears you talk to him, and he puts his hand on your face when you cry for him.

Cheyenne's reply came quickly. "You are right on! Can we do more?"

Sara sent a picture of her notes to Cheyenne to show her what she had r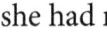

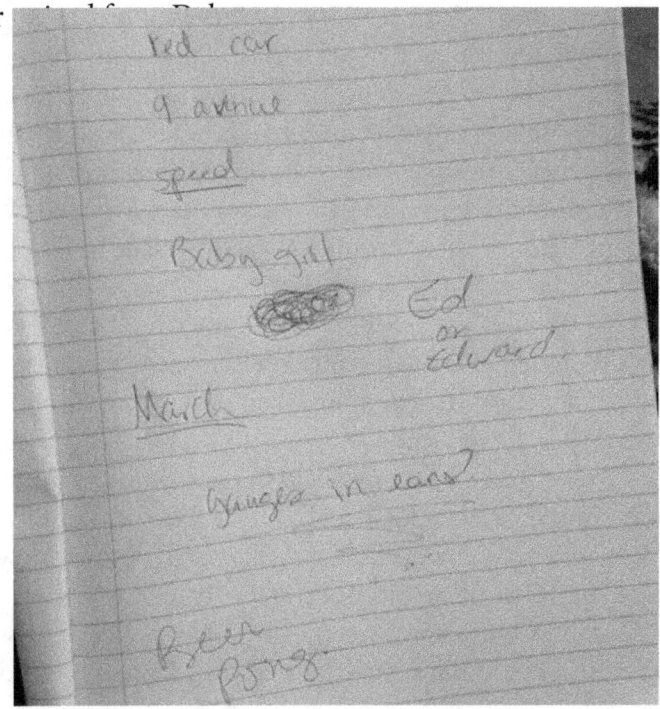

"Red car on 9ᵗʰ Avenue…was speeding. Edward is his brother. March 15 was the accident. Dakota used to gauge his ears. Beer pong was his absolute favorite." Cheyenne confirmed everything on the page with the exception of one detail and that was the mention of a baby girl. "Brittani was Dakota's good friend and is really struggling after his death." Cheyenne confirmed and added "Dakota once worked at a pizza parlor."

Sara feels the physical suffering of her clients. In this reading, she had a heaviness in her chest symbolizing the emotional and physical pain in Cheyenne's heart. The dialogue became fast and to the point.

"Cheyenne, he wants to talk about the night ya'll lay there and talked. He says he 'was goofy but he loves you.'"

"I know he loved me. I don't know what possessed him to leave. How did he know where the keys were? Why didn't he ask me to drive? Why didn't he wake me up?." Cheyenne had already related to Sara how Dakota had been drinking that night.

Even though Sara could feel Cheyenne's pain and wanted to console her, she knew her job was to let Dakota do the talking through her.

"Who puckers their lips up real big?" Sara asked smiling on her end of the FB message. "He is showing me memories."

"He did and kissed me all over my face real fast. We talked the night he died for fifteen minutes—serious face to face talk!"

"Dakota says 'I'm smart like that'—about the keys." Sara hoped Cheyenne was enjoying remembering their last playful moments together. "He has a smirk on his face when he says it."

"Oh my God!" Cheyenne's fingers work the computer keys in excitement. "He always said that!"

"Cheyenne, I've never walked in your shoes, so I'm not saying how you should or shouldn't feel, but he doesn't want you to feel guilty. It wasn't your fault. He says, 'This sucks! I can't be with you!' He wants you to know he did not suffer."

"No one will ever love me like that again. I miss him so much. I wish I could have stayed awake, but I was too tired. I heard him…yelling…I heard him yell 'FIVE, FOUR, THREE…' and I was out. I was asleep. It was like he was counting me down to sleep. And I didn't get up to see what was wrong or why he was yelling. I do wonder if he suffered. And he always said, 'smart like that'…LOL!"

"He stressed for you to stop blaming yourself. He says it was a stupid mistake that cost him his life." Sara tries hard to get Dakota's point across to Cheyenne.

"My heart hurts. Dakota is my soulmate. He is perfect and he loves me and no one will ever be like that again. I left my entire life for him and now I am alone. I miss him so much."

Again Sara's chest felt heavy, just like she was sure Cheyenne's felt every time she thought of her soulmate. Now it was time for Sara to deliver Dakota's most important message to his young wife. Sara told Cheyenne she had to speak for Dakota now and deliver his main message. Sara knew it would hurt Cheyenne, but this was what she, the messenger, had to do—her duty to those who, although passed, seek her help. She could only hope it would not be more than Cheyenne could bear. Perhaps, it would give her more sadness; perhaps, it would comfort her in her long road to recovery. Regardless, it was not Sara's message to keep but her responsibility to deliver to the one grieving.

"I have to give you this message from Dakota. It is important to him that I tell you. He said, 'That moment when our car hit the pole, it went as in slow motion, but when everything came crashing in—yes, it killed me, but I didn't feel the pain. I went numb. As the glass came in, I saw a light and I had no pain. I did, however, have flashbacks of us together. I remember running my fingers through your hair. I remember kissing your forehead and I remember your laugh. I remember you singing out loud to the radio, and I remember the love we shared together. You are the one that made my life complete, and if I could go back and relive all of our memories, bad or good, I would in a minute! But I'm gone now and you have to keep living for yourself. You are a beautiful girl—you're my beautiful wife and will always be, but I watch you lie there and cry, and I'm standing there watching you, telling you it's okay. You ask for signs. I'm here. I'm always with you.'"

"I miss him so much. I love him so much. I am so glad he said that. No one will ever be so perfect again. I know I can't spend forever alone because I'm not that type of person. I do ask for signs. I know he's here. But I want him here … here! I hate being alone so much." Cheyenne cries out from her heart.

Sara continues with the message from Dakota telling Cheyenne she will love again even though she doesn't think she can.

"Dakota says with a smirk that 'he' (*her new guy*) won't be like him but will be good for her when she's ready."

"I don't know what this means, but Dakota says to tell you 'the beer pong games are not over yet.'"

Cheyenne says she knows what it means and tells Sara about a memorial party she gave for Dakota recently. A friend of hers kept making trick shots, and everybody said it was Dakota making it happen.

Another message that kept coming through from Dakota was "baby girl", but Cheyenne could not figure this one out until it finally came to her. She explained how Dakota had lost a baby sister named Stormy in a house fire when he was young. He had tried to save her but couldn't, and he always felt guilty about it. He had a tatoo memorializing her.

Sara told Cheyenne she was sure Dakota was with his baby sister Stormy now. Another vision Sara got from Dakota was two sisters with blood on each of their fingers. They put their fingers together and Sara hears someone say "blood sisters." Later, Cheyenne found out what the vision meant. She had been contacted by the girls' new mom who had found her through Facebook, and Cheyenne was going to meet Dakota's blood sisters. Dakota had been separated from his sisters when he was adopted and had always wanted to see them again. Now Cheyenne was taking her husband's place and going to meet his birth sisters. She was sure Dakota knew this was going to happen and gave her clues through Sara.

Only a few months have passed, but as of the writing of this chapter, the grief still consumes Cheyenne most days. Sometimes she is comforted by dreams of her soulmate and best friend, and sometimes she swears she can feel him lying beside her, on the left side where he always slept. In a message, Dakota told Sara he leaves smilie faces around for his wife, and Cheyenne swears she can feel his presence, sometimes thinking she sees him. She believes he leaves written messages for her.

A few years back, Dakota wrote a poem for his grandmother who had passed away. It was a family decision to use the poem at Dakota's funeral, but now as she reads it, she can't help but think the poem was also meant for her in the unbearable present, the words fitting how Dakota felt, and still feels, about his own wife, his "beautiful, always wife."

Look into my eyes
and face what you already know.
It's time for us to say our goodbyes,
It's time for you to let me go.

Tell me that you love me
and what I've meant to you.
It's time to set me free,
Even though it's hard to do.

The years that we have shared,
Have been the best I've ever known.
I know you must be scared,
I hate to leave you here alone.

But I'll live within your heart,
When you need me I'll be there,
We will never be apart,
You will feel me everywhere.

It's pulling me away,
Bringing me into the light.
I have lived my last day,
It's my time to take flight.

- Dakota -

On the night of Dakota's death, a passerby took a picture of the wreck. Standing in the bottom of the picture is a young man looking uncannily like the young husband—even the hair is the same. Could it have been Dakota giving Cheyenne one last look at him before he "went to the light?" Are Cheyenne's dreams of her husband real? Is Dakota truly keeping watch over his grieving wife? Did Dakota really send messages to his soulmate through his personal messenger Sara? Cheyenne believes all of the above to be true. After all, her Dakota "is smart like that."

Taken by a passerby at the wreck scene: Male at front could be Dakota.

Picture of Dakota for Comparison

Soon after delivering Dakota's messages to Cheyenne, Sara received a message from Dakota's good friend Brittani thanking her for being Dakota's link and bringing his words to Cheyenne and to her.

"Hey, Brittani. It feels like I know you. I am so glad he came through for ya'll and know you and Cheyenne have been having a hard time with him gone. It breaks my heart for you. He definitely made it known he misses you, and I'm glad I was able to help in some little way." Sara then got to a new message she had just received from Dakota.

"Did ya'll dance together? He wanted to show me this memory because he cherishes it with you. It's one of his favorites."

"He doesn't normally dance, but when I took him to my family's Christmas one year, he gave me a dance game and completely lost at the game, but even if he was losing, he wasn't about to 'half-ass' it as he would have said. My whole family died laughing and taped the whole ordeal. He was dripping wet with sweat after the song. I just wish he didn't have to be my ghost and could have continued living and sharing his wisdom. He was such a bright soul." Brittani told the story, and Sara could feel the girl's emotions change from joy remembering the goofy side of her friend, to sadness thinking of Dakota as a ghost, no longer a living being.

"Dakota IS such a bright soul." Sara added.

"Thank you for sharing that with me, and thank Dakota for coming through to me as well. You, ma'am, are wonderful at what you do. I can't tell you how much I needed to connect with him."

Dakota dancing "goofy" with Brittani

A Happy Time   Dakota's Memorial Pole

Chapter Ten

The Loss of Children

What a tragedy it is to die with so much life ahead! It's not right for a child to die before the parent. It's a parent's worst nightmare! There's no greater loss than losing a child!

We have all heard and probably stated the expressions above when speaking of the death of a child, especially if they are young children. The only consolation, if there is one, is the belief as Christians that young children go straight to Jesus after dying. But unanswered questions linger long after any child's funeral is over, after the child's body has been placed in a cemetery surrounded by older family members also passed.

Do infants and young children grow up in heaven, or do they stay a child forever? Do they get to know their family members by looking down from their eternal home? Can children of any age send messages, thoughts, or feelings to their grieving loved ones on earth?

To Angel Leigh, age is not a restriction when a message needs to be carried to bring peace and comfort to a loved one. Just as in the story of Sally in Chapter Three, who wanted her mommy to know, "It's okay, Mommy", infants and small children, too, may need to send messages to those who grieve. Adult children (*sounds like an oxymoron but children in their forties or seventies are still someone's children*) have even more need to send messages, many of them with families of their own as well as grieving parents.

Following are readings for children, some who died as infants, some who died in the prime of life as teenagers, and some who died as adults. Regardless of the age of the deceased child, every parent suffers.

Tragedy? Of Course. Worst nightmare? Probably. The greatest loss? Absolutely.

Gracie Mae

Sister: This is a picture of my baby sister Gracie Mae who passed away. I don't know if you can get information about a baby since she was too young to talk when she passed, but I'd like to know if you get anything.

Sara: I'm getting the feeling that your chest is heavy, and you're having a hard time breathing. Do you have asthma?

Sister: Yes, I do.

Sara: Just make sure you have your inhaler. I don't want you stressed out. I am getting a connection. Was your sister sick when she went to sleep? Was she a SIDS baby?

Sister: Yes, she was.

Sara: I feel like she had a cold or something before all this happened, but then I feel like it was SIDS because she was sleeping so peacefully. The Lord took her before she suffered. She literally went to sleep peacefully and passed. No suffering at all. This sounds strange, but does someone drive motorcycles in your family? She says she would look like Nat or someone with that name but will have your attitude and your hair. She knows someone wondered how she would look. She also says her mama knows it was SIDS but sometimes blames herself and wonders why she didn't wake up or go to her. Her mother wonders what she could have done to save her. Please let her know Gracie Mae says she was the best mama in the world. She couldn't have saved her. Gracie Mae knows how much she was loved.

Sister: My mother drives a motorcycle, and my dad used to also. Natalie is our sister. We call her Nat.

Sara: Gracie Mae is a precious soul, and I'm glad I got to connect with her. I'm exhausted so this could be why I can't focus much. She has faded but may come back later.

Sister: You really started a healing process for me. I'm at peace. I questioned all the time what she would have been like had she got to grow up. And she would have been wonderful. But there's a reason for everything and she's okay and I'm okay. You are wonderful. Thank you so much.

Sara: She is okay. I know we question why when they are so young and didn't have a chance to live really but let her live through you and Nat. I'm always here for you if you need to talk.

A Grandmother's Lament

The refrigerator door remains filled with the same pictures that have been there far too long. All have become worn, and the magnets and tape have lost their ability to hold on like the grandmother has lost her desire to hold on to joy. The permanent marks are fading on the door facing, the growth chart that stopped forever too close to the floor. Even the children singing at church, "Jesus loves me this I know…" cause her to swallow hard as she hides her sadness and hidden anger behind a forced smile. Such can be the lament of a grandmother upon losing a grandchild.

Trudy

Sara looked at the picture of the beautiful little girl and felt an immediate bond with this grandmother who had requested a reading. As always, Sara could not imagine the grief of a parent or grandparent losing a child, especially now that she is a mom with a little boy and girl of her own.

Trudy requested a reading, hoping to connect with her

granddaughter who had died at a young age. Hopefully, this would help with her overbearing grief.

Trudy's Reading:

Sara: Hey, Trudy. She's beautiful. I'm seeing a male with her pushing her in a swing. I'm picking up a J, but don't think that is her name.

Trudy: Hi, Sara. That is probably her father John pushing her in the swing.

Sara: I see her holding a balloon and watching it float away. Did someone release balloons for her recently?

Trudy: Yes. Just a few days ago. It was her birthday.

Sara: I see her in the kitchen with frosting all over her and the cupcakes. She's laughing.

Trudy: Yes. We always made cupcakes or cookies.

Trudy answers Sara's questions giving little additional information. Sara could feel her pain but also knew Trudy was being careful not to give too much information. Perhaps she was waiting for Sara to give her something special, something only her grandchild would know. Trudy needed to feel the reading was credible; it had to be real!

Sara: She wants you to know she liked the teddy bear and wonders where it went.

Trudy: Someone stole it off her grave.

Sara: She likes to dance, 'cause she's twirling over there.

Trudy: She loved to dance!

Sara: She wants to know where her princess shoes are.

Trudy: I just bought them for her right before she passed.

Sara: This is a real tragedy. I see them going at the same time.

Trudy: Yes, it was. They went together.

Sara: I am so sorry. She hears you talk to them though. I'm glad she hears you. He wants you to know he forgives the man who killed them. They did not suffer.

Trudy: I'm glad they didn't suffer. I worry about it all the time.

Sara: I see something like proceedings in a courthouse or something. He wants you to know he was there beside you. Your chest felt as if it was caving in.

Trudy: This was the courthouse where they sentenced the drunk driver responsible for the accident.

Sara: It was a lot of sadness and anger. You walked out with a load off your chest. You looked up, smiled with tears streaming down your cheeks. This is what he is showing me.

Trudy: Yes. Exactly how it was.

Sara: She has kitten paws painted on her cheeks. Did she ever get her face painted? She says she has many children to play with now.

Trudy: She had her face painted a few minutes before the accident. I am so glad she has children to play with. Does she know about her new cousin?

Sara: She just put both of her hands up and blew a kiss. LOL.

She's fading, sweetie. They're happy and they are together.
Trudy: Did she tell you her name or initial?

Sara: She giggled 'K.'

Trudy: Yes. K. Her name is Katie. She always giggled. Thank you so much, Sara. It was beautiful.

Teenage Loss

My son's grandmother once told me, "When he's a little child, you can take him by the hand and lead him, but when he's a teenager, all you can do is pray." After raising three teenagers, I know the truth to this statement. And now, I'm seeing my children doing an abundance of praying as my grandchildren have reached those teenage years.

But even with all that leading and praying, some teenagers don't make it to adulthood. Teenagers feel they are invincible, and as parents, we are ever vigilant—watching the clock, waiting to hear the car pull into the driveway late at night, listening for the back door to slam signaling they made it through cheerleader practice, or football practice, or just out with friends. They head to the refrigerator, phone in hand, and never look up to see the worry drain from your face just at the sight of them home safe.

We also know teenagers are addicted to communication. Too bad there are no cell phones in heaven! Sara acts as a messenger for loved ones who have lost a teenage family member or friend and want to connect with them to make sure they are okay. Following you will find some readings for teenagers seeking to communicate with their loved ones through their messenger Sara.

Presley

Presley: Can you do a reading for my brother who passed?

The boy asked the question on Angel Leigh's Facebook page. The request had a picture attached. Sara looked at the picture and began writing notes.

Sara: I'm sorry about your losing your brother. He is connecting with me and says he is with someone named Cal or with a C initial. He still plays basketball every day and says he's 'the best basketball player up here.' He says to tell Mom his head doesn't hurt anymore. He talks about being transferred after the accident. There must have been some kind of a fall because he says he was numb and pain free when he fell. He knows you miss him, and he says you went anti-social for a while. He adds he is proud of you and is sorry he had to leave you and Mom.

Presley: You are right on but I don't know a Cal. *(Pause)* Oh! My Uncle Calvin! We called him Calvin. He passed away a year ago. They are together? That helps me so much. Ask him if he's happy with my life decision.

Sara: You are going to get your GED, right?

Presley: Yes. I'm getting it next school year. He was upset when I dropped out.

Sara: Well, he knows, and he is very proud of you.

Presley: That's nice to know.

Sara: He says he's always proud of you; he's your brother. He says you made it past him.

Presley: Yes. He was 17 when he passed. I'm 18. Thank you so much. Tell him I love and miss him.

Sara: He hears you and loves and misses you, too. Tell the family he loves and misses them. I know you aren't much of a believer but now can you see there are angels around you?

Presley: This helps a lot.

Sara: He is fading. I can't see him. His energy has gone for now. Your brother has your back. Get that GED.

Presley: Thank you so much. I had no idea how helpful this would be. For a year or two passed, it was tough. I was in the car he fell out of and passed away.

Sara: So now the fall and head make sense. I'm always here to help.

Randi

After I had typed in Randi's reading, dialog only, I sent it to her with the permission she needed to sign and with the reading as it would appear in the book. She sent her permission form back and asked me "So you are only putting the readings in the book and nothing about how the reading applied to our lives—just wondering."

Rinnnggg!

What a wakeup call this was for me! I was so concerned about meeting a deadline, I missed the whole reason for the readings— the human needs— the God part. Because of Randi's message, I am going back and emailing every client where I only put dialog. Shame on me! And thank you, Randi, for making me realize what was important.

In Randi's words, here is how this reading affected her life:

"Jeff was my best friend, my big brother, and the most loved person in my life. I was eleven years old when he committed suicide. He ran a hose from the exhaust into the car window, or so I was told, and they (he and his friend) cried themselves to sleep. This flipped my world upside down and I truly believe I died with him.

"At twelve years old, I started drinking and using drugs. My addiction did nothing but progress into a full-blown life style. I ate, slept, and breathed drugs, dealing drugs, and living a criminal life. I had a baby and lost her to DFCS *(Division of Family and Children Services)*. Growing up, everyone said suicide was an unforgiveable sin—straight to hell! So my whole life I believed Jeff was in hell, gone from me forever. No point in talking to him because he couldn't know what was going on; he chose to take his life and leave me here to deal with it.

"Well, after a heavy eleven years of life being high, I got to my lowest point again— pregnant, homeless, jobless, an addict—and I chose to surrender my life and commit to a rehab program where I was when I had my reading from Angel Leigh. The reading gave me so much comfort, so much closure, and so much peace within myself knowing that he's been here with me all along. Although I still don't know why, which is my heart's greatest desire, I know that he is sorry and didn't mean to. I sleep easy knowing that I was not abandoned by him all this time."

Randi's Reading

Randi: I want to know anything you can tell me about my uncle who passed. He was really more like a brother. Here's his picture.

Even though Sara was in the hospital with her grandfather and it was hard to focus, she began connecting with the young man in the picture.

Sara: Hey, Randi! He's talking about a struggle you've been through. He cried because you got saved and straightened out your life. You don't know how proud he is of you. He is so proud you stepped up, said 'I've got a problem,' and did something about it. Does this make sense?

Randi: Perfect sense.

Sara: Did his mom write something for him? He is talking about her.

Randi: I'm bawling my eyes out.

Sara: His mom misses him terribly, and he knows what she wrote. He hears what she says when she is talking to him. He says he is so sorry.

Randi: She does miss him.

Sara: He is talking about someone with the initial R but says 'Dad.'

Randi: Randy is his dad's name.

Sara: He talks about his dirt bike and about being his mom's baby.

Randi: Yes.

Sara: He keeps showing me memories of his life in images. He cherishes his memories and is smiling. He knows what you went through and how you gave your addiction to God. He takes your hand and says he was with you during it. He mentions you having a baby.

(Long pause)

Randi: Whew! I had to smoke a cigarette. Sorry.

Sara: This was a tragedy.

Randi: Yes. A complete tragedy.

Sara: I don't feel it was a car accident.

Randi: Our family hasn't been the same since he was found in the car. .

Sara: I see him giving his mama flowers to show he knows her birthday is in August. Let her know he will celebrate her birthday in heaven. He is riding his dirt bike and says he did not suffer.

Randi: I know he didn't suffer, but you have given me peace. You have been amazing. You truly are an angel. *(Pause)* Are there really angels among us, or spirits?

Sara: There are both angels and spirits but I see other things, too.

Randi: Is he an angel?

Sara: Yes, he is and he has moved on. He's in heaven. He's never been roaming the world and has always been in heaven.

Randi: You gave me so much peace. I was always told suicide was an unforgiveable sin. I always thought he was in hell. Thank you so much.

Sara: I heard he was given a second chance. He didn't go to hell. He had his moment with our Lord and Savior and he was saved.

The Loss of an Adult Child

This loss is one I know personally after losing a son at the age of forty-six, and I can assure you pain and grief are the result regardless of the age of the child. My mother who is now ninety-six years of age also lost an adult child, my sister who was thirty-four when she died. I did not understand my mother's continuing grief at that time, but I do understand it now. When losing an adult child, the grieving process is different than if he/she was a young child, but it hurts just the same.

Tracy

During a trip to Tennessee, Sara went into a quick stop for

snacks, and my friend Hilda and I sat in the car. While we sat there, I told Hilda about the one message I would love to receive more than any other through Sara.

Our oldest son Tracy had suffered from mental disease and depression and committed suicide at age forty-six. Tracy was my stepson, but I had been his second mom since he was five and I loved him dearly. The one thing that worried me the most after Tracy's death was my not knowing where he is now. Did he talk to God during his lowest point? Was he, like Randi's uncle, given a second chance?

I have a good friend Jennie who is Mormon who believes people are given a second chance to accept Jesus and her words encouraged me.

"Stop worrying about Tracy; by the time those old prophets finish teaching him, he will believe and will be okay."

Still, if Sara could get a message from Tracy, I would be reassured. I had purposely not talked about my family to Sara hoping Tracy, my sister, or my dad would make contact, but the message I had received was for my daughter-in-law. I would love to tell you Sara wrote notes about Tracy during that trip but she did not. Still, I refused to give up hope.

The next week, I got a text message from Sara.

"Do you know a Tracy?"

Sara probably wondered if I sit and stare at my phone constantly, because I texted back "yes" as soon as she hit send.

"Then this message is for you. I see him saluting and saying, 'I fought my battles. I'm at peace. I'm okay, Dad. I'm okay.' He then said, 'Hi, Jeff.'"

Tracy told me once that his stepbrother Jeff was always his hero even though Jeff was younger than Tracy. Now, Tracy had chosen Sara to deliver a simple 'Hi" to his brother. The message gave me the peace about Tracy I had wanted for three years.

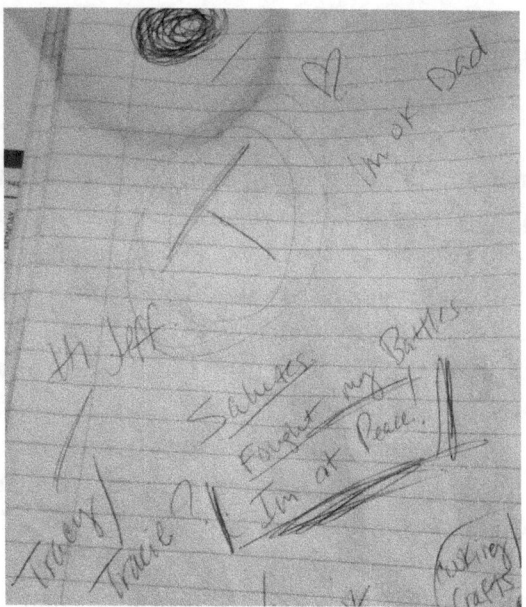

Sara's Notes From Tracy

Tracy doing what he loved

Shelly

> **Shelly:** I lost my son a little over a year ago. I pray someone connects with me. Thank you.

> **Sara:** I am so sorry for your loss. I do feel a connection, so I'm going to say what I see and hear and maybe this will make sense to you. He first wants to talk about his son. He smiles real big and says my son was everything to me. He talks about his son's foot…not sure if maybe his foot is big for his age or if he has a picture of his son's foot, but he wanted to bring that up. He will always be with his son…even though not physically, he will be in spirit, and in his son's heart. He mentioned a Rick or Ricky and says to tell him he loves him, and he knows he has his weak moments with his being gone. He said when he took his last breath, he drove away on a motorcycle. He talks of many memories. He was an outgoing and loving soul. He shows me being outdoors and always having a smile on his face, and he wants you to remember him that way. He shows me the month of June. An older female soul says she is there with him. She knows you miss him and her but they are together. He is laughing and bringing up Manda, or Amanda … around that name, and he says to please let her know he loves her so much. Lastly, he loves you and wants you to know 'I'm okay, Mom.' He asked about his dogs. Oh, he was smiling when he mentioned Manda. He seems protective of her. He talked about a baby. He said he held this baby before the baby was born if this makes sense. So the way I see it is, he passed and then a baby was born. He held the baby in heaven.

> **Shelly:** This is so spot on!!! I'm in tears! My son died in June 2014. His son was eight months old at the time. He had his son's actual footprints tattooed on his shoulder. Ricky is his dad, my husband. He has many weak moments. They were so close. He loved life! He rode his motorcycle all the time, hiked, skied, you name it! Outdoor sports for all seasons! His smile was…is contagious. The older female is my mom. They had a

super strong bond. Manda is his sister, only sibling. They were best friends and talked daily. She misses him so. His girlfriend's name is also Amanda. His dogs! LOL! Makes total sense! I gave his Spanky to his son's mom to raise with their son. We have his other one, Darla Jane. I love my son so much and miss him dearly. My breath catches most of the time when I think of him. The baby is Manda's daughter *(his niece)*. She went into labor at the funeral home and was in the hospital during the memorial service. The baby, Gemma, was born eight days after Dylan died. She was born in the same room as his son.

Sara: Well that's exactly what he was showing me. I hope if anything, this gives you just a tiny bit of peace to know he is okay. He did wonderful on validating this is him! He did say he got back right with faith and you were so proud of him for this.

Shelly: Thank you so very much! I've needed to hear this for so long. It's true. He renewed his relationship with God after his son was born. He said he needed to be a better example for his son. The pastor that helped him with this also spoke at his memorial service. Yes, I was proud of him for that move. I was always proud of him. He beat the odds so many times in his young life. It's still hard for me to believe he's gone before me. Have you heard him laugh? I listen to videos just to hear it.

Sara: He has already faded but I can say he knows how much you love him. He hears you when you talk to him and when you speak his name. You were so good to him and he was so blessed to have you as a mom. You are doing everything right. When he stepped forward to talk, he was so happy. His eyes were bright. He is okay. His soul is at peace and now he can watch over all of you. Thank you so much for the validations. That makes sense now why he was telling me about his son's foot.

Shelly: This mother's heart thanks you! God bless!!!

Dylan with his son; shows tattoo with son's footprint.

Dylan with his dog Darla Jane.

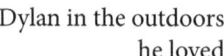
Dylan in the outdoors he loved

Chapter Eleven

A Close "Knit" Family in the United Kingdom

On a few occasions, Sara has worked with members of the same family often without knowing they are connected. This does not bother Sara, especially since she usually picks up on it when the same souls show up to deliver messages, but it is always a little confusing at the beginning.

One family in particular stands out, a family from the UK introduced to Angel Leigh by Diane. Diane has become a special client for Sara and has recommended many of her family members and friends in the UK to Angel Leigh for readings.

Sara says of this family, "I feel so close to all of them, both the living and the dead. When being contacted by those family members who are passed, I can feel their emotions, especially joy, and they come through in vivid details unlike most of the souls I encounter. They feel real to me, and I don't mean that in a negative way. I guess I should say they feel 'alive.' This family is one of the closest families I've met, and I believe that is where the energy comes from in these souls."

When the souls of this family connect with Sara, it is not usually just one; it is more like a gigantic, joyous family reunion. Sometimes Sara is overwhelmed by the size of the group but says she enjoys them immensely. She admits to being really drained after these readings since they also draw energy from her, but each experience is pleasant and very entertaining, especially if Grandpa Fred shows up and he usually does.

Included in this wonderful family are the following clients to whom Sara feels a special attachment: Diane, Angela, Selina, Rebecca, Hazel and Sarah. Sarah, the mother of twin girls Selina and Rebecca, is a strong personality, and she and her daughter Selina have an online business The Woolly Pig. *(See their website and some of their unique knitted items at the end of the chapter)*. The products on their website are full of personality just like the family members who create them. I plan to become a regular customer on their site.

This is a knitting family as evidenced by the craftsmanship in the Woolly Pig. As Diane said when talking of her mum, "My mum taught everyone of us to knit…girls, lads, kids, grandkids…I can't remember a time when she didn't knit."

As with each person whose readings are presented in this book, I sent Sarah an email with the exact way the readings will be presented in the book so she could correct anything needed and give her final approval and permission for use. Sarah sent an email to Sara, and I was so affected by her sincerity and genuineness I am adding it here:

> "Hi. How are you? Just wanted to tell you that I got Dr. Sue's email about the bit in the book and thank you for including us in it. Also, thank you both so much for having faith in the Woolly Pig. It means so much to us. XXX And now I think you met all my family, both here and on the other side: my dad, two brothers and sister, my aunts and uncles, my nannas and granddads on the other side and this side, my girls, my cousin Diane, and my mum Hazel. You made us all so very happy and I hope we will stay good friends. May God bless you always."

XXX

Now get ready to enjoy the family from the UK and their souls' adventures that include: a Rocking Chair, a Leaf Necklace, Pink Hair, a Tom Cat, Chickens, Cat, The Woolly Pig, an Open Window, and a Budweiser.

"Whew!" as Fred would say.

Diane (A Leaf Necklace, Pink Hair, Cat)

Many of Sara's clients ask her how she is able to do readings. Sara's best answer
was written to Diane who has similar abilities. Sara explained the process in the following words:

"Usually, I look at a picture and try to connect but sometimes I can't connect. When I look at a picture, other family members or close friends can also come through. Many times, once I've made a connection, I continue to get more information and images. It seems our connection gets deeper with time. And sometimes, the initial connection is all I get. When I do a reading for someone who has psychic abilities, it is sometimes harder to read, but I don't know the reason. My gift of being able to see and communicate with the dead started when I was about three, so I've dealt with it all my life, mostly trying to deny it. Only in the last few months did I begin to use my gift as I believe God intended. I am a Christian, and when I saw how I could help people and give them closure, I realized this is my calling. I hate charging for my services, but I quit my job in order to use my gift full time. My real name is Sara, but since I see angels and my middle name is Leigh, I decided on Angel Leigh for my Facebook page."

When Sara realized Diane has gifts similar to her own, she helped Diane to understand the gift and also told her how to protect herself, just in case she runs into negative energy. This is something a person with this gift doesn't like to think about but it can happen.

"Your say you heard two people and one said, 'Hey' totally makes sense to me. It is like it is coming through your mind even though you can sometimes see images. It can be scary and something you are afraid to acknowledge. You know in your heart you have this gift and just know something is a little different. I want to try to understand what you see and hear, or even feel so we can figure out what type you are and how to help you control it and become stronger. Do you know how to protect yourself? My friend Kate who is a paranormal investigator taught me how to protect myself. I imagine I'm in a relaxing place; then I imagine a white light surrounding me. Do you see images in your mind or with your eyes? I see both and sometimes feel like it's a moving picture. Write it all down even if it doesn't make sense."

In Diane's reading, Sara picked up many things including: military backgrounds in some family members, one older male soul with tattoos; a necklace having what looked like an angel wing on it and a male soul touching it and smiling. Many souls appeared in this reading. Here is some of the dialogue:

Sara: Do you own a feather necklace? Early this morning, I was lying there and I saw a male soul come up and touch a feather or angel wing necklace of yours. He looked at it and smiled.

Diane: I did have a necklace that was a dream catcher with two angel wings but they fell off. I have a silver necklace with a leaf that could be taken for an angel wing. I had several older family members in the military and some had tattoos. My husband has lots and so does his brother. Did he say who he is, the one touching the necklace?

Sara: No, he doesn't say his name. I'm seeing a baby boy with a name beginning with an E…a different name like Euine. He is the baby boy born sleeping.

Diane: Yep. Euan is spot on for one.

Sara: Does someone collect dolls? And does someone knit?

Diane: My mum and Cat. Now Cat still collects dolls.

Sara: They like to bring up little things. It validates they are who I say they are. Did someone hurt in the legs? I see someone rubbing their legs and they are having trouble walking.

Diane: My mum used to rub her legs. She had trouble walking. My mum taught every one of us to knit…girls, lads, kids, grandkids…I can't remember a time when she didn't knit. LOL. And yes she was a doll collector. Take care and bless you for all your hard work. You will never know what it means to me… each day getting one step further. Thank you.

Here is part of another reading for Diane:

Sara: I'm trying to connect but a dark haired little girl says to tell you she loves you. She is saying, "I'm Kelly." She is saying she is with him if that makes sense. There is an older lady and man. I sense your parents but not 100% sure. They are saying they have the sweet baby boy and he's okay. Does this make sense?

Diane: Every single bit makes sense, Hun. Not sure why Kelly is around him apart from kids loved being around him. LOL.

Sara: I'm getting a C but I don't know if this is him.

Diane; Yes, the photo is Craig.

Sara: Okay, that's him that is coming through. He's with several and he's okay. He mentions his brother and that he's okay, too, and not suffering.

Diane: Thank you. I have lost many family members and friends and am glad they get together. XXX

Sara: I was making contact with Craig earlier. So there was a little dark haired girl around him. They are all together. She is older now…like she passed away young but it's been a long time since she passed.

Diane: I couldn't understand why she was with him, but why not? I knew them both. LOL. Kelly passed when she was 9 and it will be 19 years ago in December.

Sara: He does make it confusing. Was it your nephew or son?

Diane: Nephew.

Sara: He shows me you loved him like a son.

In another reading, Sara talks to Diane about an older soul rocking the baby Euan. The older soul brings up someone but he's mentioning her having like wild colored hair…she is very confident and her name starts with A. Like Angie or something. He says they are very close and he watches over her and he is okay.

Diane: Another 100%, Hun.

Diane tells Sara this is her daughter Angela who dyes her hair bright pink all the time.

Angela
Angela is the daughter of Diane, the one with pink hair, and another member of this wonderful family. Angela seems to know how Sara's visions work and tells her, "Here is a picture of a loved one that has passed, but I'm more than happy to hear from anyone… whoever comes through or anything you get would be appreciated."
Each time Sara sends me a reading from this family to use in the book, I get excited and secretly hope Fred will show up. I really want to see if my image of him is real.
Sara had just come back from her first trip to Adams, Tennessee on a field investigation and was mentally drained. She had a hard time focusing but gave Angela what she received.

Sara: I was going to try to focus and see if I could help you, but I don't know if this one is for you. I do have an older female soul

but she is the one that said she hurts in her legs and feet a lot.
Angela: Yes, that makes sense to me. That is her in the photo.

Sara: Okay. It can be confusing at times. Let me tell you what I am seeing. It could be several I'm picking up. I only see cancer, so someone that is connected to you passed of some type of cancer. Also, this beautiful lady mentions a baby. She asked how the baby is.

Angela: Yes, a few in the family died of cancer. I had a baby not long ago. He's well, thank you.

Sara: Then I hear a Nen, or Nan. Sorry but sometimes it comes through this way.

Angela: One of my grandmas was called Nen by other grandkids but not me…a different one from the photo.

Sara: Great! I was hoping there was a connection. Nen is there with her.

Angela: They did know each other alive and chatted when they would meet.

Sara: One is knitting. I wish I knew how to do that.

Angela: That's a deffo! She was always knitting.

Sara: I get overwhelmed…sorry. A male is there also. I've actually had him come through before. He says he is your brother. I think he is referring to looking at you as his sister. Is this Craig? Do you know him? He said he was your brother and smiled.

Angela: I know who you mean…he's not my brother but I saw him as one. Yes, it's Craig. We were very close.

Sara: He does love you and he knows you have your weak moments. The lady steps forward and talks of a wedding. Says there is going to be one and wants you to know she will be there for it. Goodness! Hope this makes sense. It could mean you found the one.

Angela: I do have weak moments. There was talk of me getting married. Others are getting married, so it could be any of five weddings. LOL.

Sara: She mentions you.

Angela: It must be mine. Bout time!

Sara: She said she will be there for your beautiful time so it is you.

At this point, it seems Nen knows more than Angela since she hasn't set a date yet. Angela tells Sara to ask Nen if she knows when it is. Nen replies only with a wink letting Angela know she approves. Angela agrees that "he is a good lad", and Nen talks about him bringing her granddaughter flowers.

Sara: There's an older male with her. Did her husband pass?

Angela: Yes.

Sara: They are together. Did he have breathing problems? He talks of having a hard time breathing and being short winded, something chest related. He says he is okay now. He's where he wants to be…with her.

Angela: It sounds like my other granddad.

The reading becomes confusing here as to which set of grandparents are coming through. Sara explains how it isn't always clear and often sounds like a Walkie Talkie with many souls coming through. She asks if Angela knows a Peg or Peggy. When Angela does not know one, Sara suggests it could be the grandmother suggesting baby names.

Sara: She keeps talking of how you are a great mommy. Did you have a hard time picking a baby name?

Angela: Yes. He was five weeks old before he got a name. LOL.

This grandmother may have passed on, but she is one hundred percent grandmother and watches over her daughter and grandchildren. She talks of how Angela's daughter looks just like Angela, and then gives a grandmotherly warning telling Angela to make her daughter stop taking pictures with her stomach showing. Angela laughs at this and validates the picture taking. During the conversation, Sara asked if Angela had a cat. Angela suggested she was talking about her daughter who goes by the nickname Cat. The grandmother wants Cat to know she mentioned her. At this point, Sara realizes Angela is connected to Diane, Sara's client who brings many clients to Angel Leigh. Angela is added to the book as part of this wonderful family. As the grandmother fades, Sara apologizes for not being focused and getting a clear reading. She promises to do better in the future and says she will contact her if anything else comes through.

Angela: Wow! If that's not your 100%, I can only imagine just how good you are…That's a true gift!

Hazel

Hazel was another family member of Diane and Sarah's who requested a reading and sent two pictures of ladies. Sara felt a connection but had to explain how sometimes the ones who come through are not necessarily the ones the client requests. Sara went ahead with the reading and hoped it all was meaningful to Hazel.

Sara: I hope I make the right connection and, hopefully, some of this will make sense. I feel I've seen some of these beautiful souls before. First there's an older male soul…tall guy…taps his stomach when he laughs and says, "My wife fed me good." I feel his name is an F initial…He's a funny guy. He says, "I'm here with our kids. I sense another male with him but then I see two babies. He says, "We are all together and we are okay." He wants you to know he was with you during your fall or some type of accident and held your hand. He says you are a tough one. He made sure you were okay before leaving you. I do pick up a female who likes to knit and make things with her hands. She's extremely crafty.

Hazel: I thank you for the reading. It was spot on. The man was Fred my husband. Yes, we lost two babies and a grown up son. Yes, I did have a fall in the bath and I know someone was there helping me as I felt so calm at the time.

Sarah's Family

What a novel, Sarah's story would make! I emailed Sarah and asked her to send me some pictures of her family and to tell me about herself. Somehow, I knew there was a wonderful story behind this lady who was able to make me laugh through her readings with Angel Leigh. *(I will refer to Sara as Angel Leigh to keep from confusing the two names, Sara and Sarah).* The first thing Sarah told me was, "I am deaf." Angel Leigh had already told me Sarah was deaf, but Sarah did not know Angel knew. Here is the story of how, once again, Angel Leigh was validated, this time through Nana.

While Angel Leigh was envisioning Fred and other family members back in July as she did readings for the family clients, an older woman with a soft voice and a sweet smile came into the background. She looked at Angel Leigh and said, "I'm Nana." Nana showed up each time, but the last time, Nana moved her lips without speaking and formed the words "I love you", a message for her granddaughter. When Angel asked why she did not speak aloud, Nana put her fingertips to her mouth, brought it down and shook it and then put her hand to her ear, brought her hand down and shook it, sign language for being deaf. When an image of Sarah came before Angel Leigh, she knew what it meant. Sarah is deaf.

Being the tenderhearted person she is, Angel Leigh never mentioned to Sarah about knowing she was deaf and Sarah never told her. Angel told Sarah her Nana said she loves you.

When Sarah was just a small child, her mother Hazel gave birth to Philip but was very ill with the new baby. Sarah's dad Fred worked on the farm and just could not take care of Sarah. This is when Sarah went to live with Nana and never left.

"I was always very close to my dad Fred," wrote Sarah. "He could not read or write very good, but he used his hands and made things. He was a farmer, a bricklayer, made shoes—you name it, Dad could do it. Mum says we all got a bit of Dad in us."

Sarah wrote how she only hears low whispers but learned to read lips as a child. She did not know she was deaf until she had her twin girls Selina and Rebecca. The doctors told her she had probably been deaf since birth and just adapted to her disability. Sarah said people told her she talked like a deaf person but she didn't know how that sounds.

Sarah wrote, "I was told I would never have children, but a few years after and a year to the day my Nana died, I was told I was going to have a baby." Later, a scan showed twins and Sarah said she "smiled all that day." Sarah went to college but carried her two-year-old twin girls with her there and everywhere she went. She worked as a nursery teacher but had to stop work because of health issues. Sarah and her daughter Selina started The Woolly Pig as an online business and they do well, especially at Christmas, Sarah's favorite time of the year. *(Pictures of Sarah's family and others can be found at the end of Sarah's reading along with information about The Woolly Pig).*

Selina

The first of Sarah's family to contact Angel was Sarah's

daughter Selina who sent a picture of a loved one with a request for a reading. Since Selina was rushed for time, as well as being afraid she would lose her connection, Sara went through what she was getting in one long message.

> **Sara:** First, he's with someone else, another male soul who is the main one I'm getting, either Bert or Al or even Albert. He is an older soul and is asking how your sister is. He says there are two of you. He talks about a move and how proud he is of you. I feel his death was heart related because he points to his chest. A longhaired dog is with him. He talks of you and your sister wearing matching outfits and keeps talking about the month of June as a very special month. He is handing me red roses. He needs you to know he is okay and is finally pain free, and he wants you to know he will always be with you.

> **Selina:** My dad is Albert, called Barrie. I moved in June. I am a twin. He died of a heart attack. He had a dog. June is my birthday, and I got red roses for my birthday. Wow! Perfect validation! Thank you so much!

> **Sara:** One more thing I am picking up is a baby. Someone lost a baby boy, and I am getting an N for his name. Thought this might be important.

> **Selina:** My Nan lost a baby boy Nigel.

> **Sara:** Please tell her Nigel is with loved ones.

Rebecca

Next in the family, Rebecca asked for a reading, wanting to connect with her dad. She sent her own picture and a picture of her dad, and Sara got a connection as soon as she looked at them. Rebecca also had some questions about her future, but Sara explained how she connects with those passed and really doesn't do predictions or give advice for the future. With this said, Sara begins the reading.

Sara: I am seeing a male soul step forward, and he says to tell Mom it was him with the window. Not sure what that means, but he keeps saying he visited and left the window or door open, and it scared someone. I keep picking up Berrie or Barrie, and there is another soul with him—actually a few souls are with him. I feel shortness of breath and a pain in my chest. I'm not sure if this is your dad, but I feel this person passed from heart problems.

Rebecca: Yes. That is how my dad passed. I remember when we found the window open. It scared Mum and me because we didn't know how it happened.

Sara: I see an older female with him and the name Vera or a V name comes in. When he mentioned a baby, he said, 'He's like one of my grandbabies', but I'm not sure what that means. He talks of how proud he is of you. There is a male with them. Drew, maybe Andrew or something like that. He laughs and says, 'Hey, I'm just fine.' A woman with short gray hair says, 'I'm Nana.' They are all around each other so your dad is not alone. He's with family, and he's okay. He's pain free, healthy, and happy.

Rebecca: Wow! This is all making sense! I'm amazed!

Sara: I'm picking up two people. The first man is an older soul, maybe the man in the picture. He has his hands in his pockets and is wearing denim overalls. He keeps saying, 'Whew! I'm outside!' I keep getting an F for his name. He is telling stories and enjoying it. Fredrick or Fred is coming through. He says, 'Hey. I'm with Ken!'

Sara visualizes this in full color details, something unusual. The scene is very green with a pond in it. It is a farmer's heaven and Fred was a farmer.

Rebecca: That's my granddad Fred and Ken is Mom's uncle.

Sara: He keeps talking about chickens running around or something like that. *Sara chuckled at the image of Fred with chickens running around him.*

Rebecca: My mum said, 'Yes, on chasing chickens.' I am shocked at how this is all coming through.

Sara: Perfect! I'm glad the chickens make sense. I thought you might think I was a crazy woman talking about chickens! I see V knitting, cooking, and doing for everyone else.

Rebecca: It's got to be Vera!

Sara: Vera says she has Andrew. I see the word cancer, not sure why. He shows me the month of November, puts his head down, and says to tell Cam he's sorry and he's proud of him. Does this make sense?

Rebecca: Yes, it does.

Sara: I see the word Budweiser, but no explanation.

Rebecca: That I don't know about.

Sara: I know this all came at you at once, but that was the way I got it—a lot of strong souls there.

Rebecca: That's fine. This all makes sense except for the Budweiser. I'm truly amazed!
Rebecca assures Sara she was on the right track even though many souls came at her at once.

Sara: Sometimes, I see so many different images, it all runs together. I'm glad it all made sense.

Sara could have said "Whew!" like Fred at this point. So many souls in one scene but so much fun and love!

Sarah: (Rocking Chair, Tom Cat, Woolly Pig, and Budweiser)

Sarah asked for a reading after her cousin Diane recommended Angel Leigh. Sarah writes as if she is nervous since she has never done this before but sends pictures of herself and the deceased ones with whom she hopes to contact.

After looking at the pictures, Sara makes a connection and begins Sarah's readings. *(I hope the "Sara" and "Sarah" are not too confusing).*

Sara: I have made a connection. First, let me say how sorry I am for your loss. I hope I am making the right connection. I pick up Nana, or that is what she calls herself. She is holding a baby boy and says you are his sister—Big Sis at that, and she wants you to know the baby boy is okay. She's rocking him, and he has his fingers in his mouth. I also pick up a male who feels like more of a brother to you. I pick up Drew. What's crazy is I have seen his image before and feel like he has come through another time. I see two other guys, older males standing there with the older female soul. He watches over you. He makes me feel like he's your dad because he's very protective of you. Did your husband pass? Also, there's a female baby, initial D. There is so much coming that it's overwhelming! Maybe you can validate some or all of this and let me know. They are all together and at peace. One mentions a cat and also says to tell your girls he loves them. This is all I'm getting but maybe this will help you in some way to know they're watching over you. God bless.

Sarah: Yes, thank you. My Nana is one I miss so much and the baby boy is my little brother Nigel. He was a year old when he died. Drew is my brother Andrew who died last year. You have seen Andrew before in a reading for someone else. Yes, it could be my dad. I miss him so much and he was very protective of me. My husband has not passed as I know, but my girls' dad who was older than me, has and the cat is my best cat Tom. The female baby is my older sister Denise who died at six months. I was born the year she died and never got to see her but was told I look just like her. I expected you'd get lots coming. I am a family history teacher and everyone I find, I feel a bond with, if that makes sense. And yes, I have twin girls, Rebecca and Selina, who have had readings from you. Thank you so very much. All you said is correct, and all I wanted to know is that they love me. I love them all and miss them. No one loves me here but my girls. Sorry for that last bit. Wish you all the best in what you do. Take care and God bless you. Thank you.

Sara: I'm glad they came through for you. I was wondering about Drew. Yes, they watch over you and love you so much. Your Nana is with you always. She was rocking in a chair and saying 'I'm Nana.' She's proud to say it. Just always know they love you because you are an amazing person and mother. I'm glad things were validated for you.

Sarah: Oh! By the way! *Sarah (the client) stops Sara (the messenger) from closing.* My Nana always wanted a rocking chair and never got one. Looks like now she has. Bless her!

Before the reading ended, Sarah thanked Sara for doing the readings for her twin daughters. She also thanked her for putting Rebecca's mind at ease. Rebecca had been late for her dad Barrie's funeral and never forgave herself. Getting his message put her mind at ease.

"Oh!" Sarah adds one more remark before closing. "And just to let you know, Andrew was the one who said 'Budweiser' because it was his favorite drink."

The Woolly Pig: Hand Knitted
https://www.facebook.com/thewoollypig

Fred

Hazel

Sarah with Fred

Fred and Hazel

Angie with her pretty pink hair

Diane with granddaughter Cat.
Diane wearing her leaf necklace

Sarah and her twin girls Selina and Rebecca

Chapter Twelve

More Readings

     Angel Leigh feels every reading she does is of the utmost importance. When she makes a connection and brings a message to a loved one, she has done what God wants her to do. The readings in this book are by no means all of the people Sara has helped. When posting on her page and asking if anyone wanted to be included in the book, she was given permission by almost all, but unfortunately not all could be included.

     All of Sara's clients are important, and she worries about not being able to add all who wanted to be included in the book. She really doesn't like the word "client" feeling it is too impersonal, something Sara could never be. Besides, Sara keeps in touch with most as if they are old friends.

Barbie   Stephanie   Tracye

This book would not be complete without including the first family Sara helped. Sara had just accepted her gift and gone public with her Angel Leigh page when Tracye contacted her. Sara communicates with the family so much that she could fill a book on them alone. Following is a summary of readings, some in Sara's words, for this special family.

"A sweet girl named Tracye wrote me asking if I could connect with her aunt who died very young. I started picking up a beautiful female with the prettiest eyes I have ever seen but it was Tracye's cousin. She talked of her kids, a boy and a girl, and showed me memories of herself lying in a hospital bed and being stuck with so many needles, another cancer horror story.

"The cousin showed me her brother who had passed first, and she wanted her mother to know he took her hand and welcomed her when she took her last breath. I talked of the brother's tattoos, a favorite black hat, of his artistic talent, of items placed in their caskets such as a gold ring, all of this being the souls giving information for validation so their family would know it was they speaking through me.

"When the aunt came through, she talked about how she liked her niece's hair that had just been dyed and how much she liked the flowers that had been put on her grave. Her aunt talked about a baptism coming up, her daughter's, and how important this dedication was to her. Tracye was happy that her aunt and cousins had sent messages.

"A week later, I got a request for a reading from another pretty lady named Barbie, Tracye's sister, who was pregnant. I immediately saw two babies who had passed. These babies had been Barbie's, and now Barbie was pregnant again and praying this baby would make it. She had a beautiful baby boy with a great delivery.

"Then Stephanie wrote me, and I found out the three were sisters. I not only message these sisters but we call each other. They are family, my first family to help using my gift, and I will always feel close to them."

Stephanie called Sara one night and told her every time she

started to text her, she got this overly hot sensation all over her body and she could not understand it. Sara could not explain it, but it could have meant she and Stephanie had a strong connection.

Sara knew Stephanie wanted to have a baby more than anything and Sara told her she sees her with a beautiful baby girl. Stephanie believes in Sara so this was wonderful news. In Stephanie's family, there is a ten-year-old boy who shows signs of having the same gifts as Sara. Since he was just a small child, he would walk up to a woman, point, and say, "You are going to have a baby, and it will be a _____." The woman would not even know she was pregnant but would later find out she was, and when the baby was born, it would be the gender the boy had foretold. Stephanie said the boy is never wrong. After Sara told her she would have a baby girl, the boy came up to her one day and told her she would have "the prettiest baby girl." Stephanie was so excited to have both Sara and the boy tell her the same thing.

Sara also did a reading for Stephanie's husband, describing a large unusual necklace his grandfather had worn before he passed. With all that Sara told him, she turned a nonbeliever into a believer.

Sara feels so close to this family and has done readings for almost all of them. She says, "Some day, I want to visit this family and meet them in person. I feel so close to them, but especially I want to meet the boy with the gift and help him to understand his fears. I have talked to him on the phone, and I had flashbacks the whole time I was talking to him. He even sees blue bubbles."

Nicole

Sometimes, messages are jumbled, but Sara spits them out as she hears them in hopes they will make sense to the loved one. Just such a message came through for Nicole.

Sara: I was just curious if any of this makes sense LOL…Cee Cee…tomato gravy…D initial with a heart…said he was proud of her and she is looking good. Also, a birthday or anniversary for D in November because he hands her flowers. *(Sara then remarks her phone is dying).*

Nicole: OMG! PLEASE TELL ME MORE! My heart just dropped!!! OMG! I'm speechless!

Sara: That's all I'm getting at the moment. I wanted to make sure I had the right connection because two people came through.

Nicole: Every single bit of that makes sense.

Sara: I'm glad. The other is like a brother maybe to the D initial, Diane or Diana or around that name.

Nicole: Diane it is.

Sara: Okay. I thought I was wrong. LOL. That's all I have right now.

Nicole: No. You're definitely not wrong. You are right on… Oh my goodness, yes, girl, you are all over it…Right on! I have tears of joy if you know more, please text me any time of day or night.

Sara: Just know he's okay and he's with others, especially this other guy. I hope I didn't freak you out.

Nicole: No, you didn't freak me out at all. Thank you so much. You have been such a blessing to me. I am still speechless about the reading on my precious daddy. I love and miss him terribly! I believe the other man is my uncle but I don't know for sure.

Not long after doing Nicole's reading and late at night while Sara was asleep, she was awakened by a message on her phone. Feeling it was important, she went to her phone and read the following message from Nicole.

Nicole: Sara, I don't know if you are in bed or not, but I've got to tell you this. God has got my attention through you. He placed me in the right place at the right time so that I could meet you…I can't explain to you how thankful I am and how this has changed my life in so many ways. It's changed my attitude, my thinking, my everything. I'm so at peace I don't even worry anymore which is a true blessing. I worry so badly about everything. I am such a better person through you somehow. God works in mysterious ways and I'm back to who I am. I'm forever grateful. I just had to get this off my chest.

Jessica

Jessica is Nicole's friend. Her reading with Angel Leigh brought her an immense feeling of relief. Here is her story in her own words.

"I struggled for seven years with infertility, and the month we found out that my mother was critically ill with cervical cancer, I also found out I was pregnant. Throughout my entire pregnancy, I was taking care of my mother. My daughter was born in May, and I lost my mother in August, and less then a month later I found out I was pregnant again. My mother had said once when I was struggling to conceive, that if it took her dying for me to be able to be a mother, then she would gladly go be with GOD. So at the time of me being a new mom to a daughter and pregnant with my son, I lost the one that should have been there to help me through all the ups and downs of not knowing what to do. Then when everything seemed to be going good, my sister was also diagnosed with cervical cancer. She fought for three years but to no avail. She also passed.

"Angel Leigh's reading gave me the peace I needed to know my mom and sister are together, doing well, and are still keeping their eyes on all of us. They were always the ones that I went to for anything and everything. Losing them both to the same disease was very tough. Now I feel relief knowing that they are happy and always around. I never had that sense of "someone is watching over me" until they passed away. Now I get that feeling from time to time, and I know without a doubt, the feelings I have are true. It is them letting me know they are still here with me."

Jessica's mom Linda

Jessica's reading

Jessica: I am Jessica, Nicole's friend. I'm sending you a picture to see if you can give me any information. Thank you.

Sara: I do feel a small connection, so I'm gonna just say what I feel and see and hope I have the right lady. She mentions restoring her car…She says 'you should have seen it', and she talks of how good it looked. She mentioned a VW type car and laughs when she says it. She is showing me her memories. She talks of the man that loved to restore them…Glenn. She talks of hearing you when you talk to her and knows how much you miss her. Did you go back to college? She talks of an accomplishment and how proud she is. There's another female with her and an older male who says he is a grandfather. The female talks of water and then smiles. Her name starts with a T and is unique. I can't quite understand her but it is Tywa or Tyila or around that. She's okay and is happy. She talks of the 4th of July for some reason. All of them are together. I feel the beautiful lady in the picture could be your mother. She wants you to know she's proud of you and her grandkids. Is someone a teacher? She talks of you being a great mom and always at school functions. She talks of a necklace, but I'm not sure if she wanted you to have one that was hers or something. Just always know she's in your heart and is at peace. If I get anything else,

I'll let you know.

Jessica: Um! Everything you mentioned was dead on. Wow! I'm amazed! Thank you so much. I called my father Glenn and read this to him. When I got to the part about Twyla, my sister, he lost it and was a crying mess. He's a nonbeliever of anything and everything so for him to react like that was simply a miracle. So thank you! Yes, you definitely had the right person!!!! It was all things that related to us.

Sara: I'm so glad it did. I'm a Christian and everything I do is through faith and God. I'm not a medium; I'm a messenger. I struggled with this my whole life; why was I able to see things others couldn't. Then one day I prayed and asked God to lead the way. Since then, I've helped hundreds throughout the world with grief and closure. You will have to read my book. It explains everything.

Jessica: I will!!! God has blessed you and may he keep blessing you with the power to help others. The picture was of my mom Linda. My sister was Twyla. I guess I didn't tell you that. My dad is Glenn and he did restore antique cars. My mom had an old '69 VW bug she loved when I was born.

Heather

Sara tells those who request a reading that she only needs a picture and no information. Even names aren't wanted. "The less information you give, the better," Sara says, "That's how I validate." Heather sent a picture and a connection was made.

Sara: With the picture, I'm getting Rod or Rodney. If this is him, just let me know so I know I have the right person.

Heather: Yes, that's him. Rodney.

Sara: I get the month of February, and he shows me flowers.

Heather: That's when he passed.

Sara: I'm getting another man with the initial D. Then there's an older woman and she's cooking for him.

Heather: His dad was Donald or Don. He's definitely a food lover. LOL.

Sara: He wants everyone to know he's okay and it (*heaven*) is everything people talk of.

Heather: I think of him all the time. Today, I said, "Dad, please connect with this lady for me."

Sara: I'm so glad he did. Do you have boys? He talks of someone named Logan.

Heather: I do. Logan is my youngest. Do I tell you the oldest name?

Sara: No. I'm hoping he will tell me. Does one like super heroes because he talks of that. And yes, you do make him proud, he says.

Heather: OMG! I asked him that the last time I was at his grave.

Sara: He hears you talk to him.

Sara: He talks of someone that sounds like Carolyn. He says he misses her.

Heather: My stepmother is Carol, his wife.

Sara: Do you know if he danced with someone at a wedding or a big celebration? He's showing me him dancing with a brown haired woman. He says, 'I don't dance so that's a big deal.'

Sometimes I see flashes of memories he wants me to see. That's one of his best memories.

Heather: I hope he's talking about my wedding. I have brown hair and that's my favorite picture of us because we were laughing.

Sara: Perfect! That's one of his best memories. He hears you talk to him. I'm glad I got your answer.

Heather: Me, too. Thank you so much.

Sara: C…he says C. He says the boys need to help their momma more. LOL. He is very proud of all of you and your boys. I am getting Cole. He loves ya'll.

Heather: Cole is my oldest.

Sara: When I hear him it's muffled sounding but that's how I hear them usually. He keeps saying he's okay.

Heather: Good! I was super worried about that for a long time. Then I started getting little signs and it made me feel like he was okay.

Sara: He was kind of shy at first but afterwards he talks and tells stories. I'm so glad he picked that up about the wedding. Always know he's with you. And yes, very proud of you.

Heather: You don't know how much this means to me. Thank you so much.

Sugar

Sugar asked for a reading on her dad who had passed away. Sara got a connection but it was with someone named Arcade. Sugar responded telling Angel Leigh this was her mother's father who passed seven years ago. This sometimes happens. Others who are with the loved ones will sometimes step in and give messages of their own. The souls are anxious to let their loved ones know they are okay and happy. In this case, Arcade wanted Sugar to know he was with her father. Then Angel Leigh mentions Anthony.

Sugar: My baby is Anthony.

Angel: He mentions something about someone with mouth problems. And are you getting married?

Sugar: My mom just got dentures after twenty years. Yes, I am getting married.

Angel: He says he will be there to walk you down the aisle. Who is Pauly or Pauline?

Sugar: My mom.

Angel: He says no matter what, he loved her. He didn't express his feelings as he should, but she was a hard worker and he needs her to know he loves her.

Sugar: Yeah. He wasn't very good at showing his emotions or feelings.

Angel: Do you know a Mary Jane or Mary Jean?

Sugar: Mary Jean is my aunt and Jean is my grandmother. Both are still living.

Angel: Okay. The Arcade soul said Mary Jean.

Sugar: That was his wife. My grandparents.

Angel: He said to tell her he sends bluebirds her way and to look for them. Did your dad fish? I keep seeing water and I'm not sure why.

Sugar: He did some but broke his back in the water and it caused a long roller coaster of bad things for him.

Angel: Oh, so that is why I see water. Was someone talking of spreading his ashes in water? He keeps mentioning the water.

Sugar: Yes, my brother wanted to put both parents' ashes together and let them go on the water but my mom said no to that idea.

Angel: Also someone had stomach problems, maybe cancer or something but I keep picking up stomach problems. Both parents?

Sugar: That's how he died…was stomach related. They think gallbladder cancer.

Sara: Your dad keeps talking about the water idea. He likes it. I know your mom is not ready to let him go, but one day he will meet her again.

Sugar: I was wanting to take my family to the ocean to restart a 4th of July tradition that my dad started when I was a kid. I couldn't afford to pay for it. Maybe that's it.

Sara: Did they have some type of car he talked about? Because he said he would drive up and get her in it. LOL. Not sure which type car but he said that. Oh, that could be it! Sometimes I get these images and messages and they don't make sense. I have to figure out what it means. That could be it. He wants to talk about your kids.

Sugar: Good. I was hoping so.

Sara: This guy stepped forward and is raising your kids? He shows me someone not being there for you and then this man comes along and you and him have a baby now.

Sugar: Yes. 100% right.

Sara: He wants him to know he gives him all respect for taking care of you and your kids. Not all men do that and in his eyes, he is a good man. He gives his hand for him to marry you.

Sugar: Thank you.

Sara: He has some dog with him, also. He says, 'It's not as fat as the cat?' Do you own a fat cat? LOL.

Sugar: Yes. LOL! He always called her fat girl. The letter J you got in the beginning was probably his beloved Jimi, his bulldog he had.

Sara: He says your daughter saw him after he passed. He talks of her hair getting wild. He loves it though. Hope this makes sense.

Sugar: Yes. The two girls are mixed with Afros.

Sara: Precious. I bet they are beautiful. He says he bets it was rough on Father's Day. He's so sorry.

Sugar: Yes. I cried all day.

Sara: He knows and he hears you talk to him. He said to tell Kelli hello. Who is Kelli?

Sugar: OMG! My cousin Kelli is coming from Florida on

Monday.

Sara: He talks of his death. He said that he was right with God and he got to meet Jesus himself.

Sugar: Oh? I'm shocked because he was not religious.

Sara: I'm sorry. I don't usually talk about religion, but he said it, so I had to say it.

Sugar: I have gone back and forth unsure for years if there is a God or not. And tried church a few times with my kids.

Sara: Maybe that's why he needs you to know.

Sugar: Wow!

Sara: I'm not pressuring you or anything. I'm just letting you know what he is saying. I didn't know you wondered if there was a God, but now it makes sense why he said it. He wants you to know there is one. He said he missed the cake.

Sugar: All the time I bake with my girls. Or maybe the huge cake I got on my daughter's birthday. She was so sad her Grampy wouldn't be there for her first 'big girl party.'

Sara: Aw! Let her know he was there in heart.

Sugar: That was the cake for sure. He never missed a birthday party for my kids no matter how sick he was.

Sara: That's a good man. He said something about a big glass of milk.

Sugar: He always has a glass of milk with his cake. Could you ask him why he passed before we got married? I was supposed to get married that afternoon. Had a justice of the peace going to the hospital so I could include my dad.

Sara: He says it was out of his control. That's why he wanted you to know he would be there walking you down the aisle. You deserve that wedding.

Sugar: Ok. I needed that. You knew things that you couldn't have looked up anywhere or known unless you truly did connect. I am forever grateful to you. I needed this more than I can say. You are truly gifted.

Sherrie and Carol

Sara connected with Sherrie's daughter Carol first and then connected with Sherrie. Sara received mental pictures of Sherrie's mom in a hospital bed, surrounded by people laughing and talking and she had a tube in her throat. The mother wanted Sherrie to know she was okay and this message brought Sherrie great comfort.

Sherrie and her mom having fun

"I somehow became deeply connected with Sherrie and her daughter Carol and one day after getting a weird feeling, messaged them to see if they were okay. Sherrie told me she was in the hospital with Carol who was hurting really bad in her stomach. Sherrie's mom came through again and asked me if I liked her blue dress. I could see and smell white flowers. She talked about candy, and I could see she had something in her mouth. Later, Sherrie confirmed her mom was buried in a blue dress and white flowers were used at her funeral. Butterscotch candy was her mom's favorite, and she always kept it in her mouth.

Sara is still good friends with Sherrie and Carol and often sees their day to day homes, but the strangest thing about their friendship is Sara always knows when either of them is sick or in the hospital.

Kathleen

Just being in the presence of a person whether Sara knows them or not can trigger a connection with a soul. One such incident happened at Sara's house while visiting with two young girls, one being her cousin.

"I was sitting on the couch with my cousin Mary Grace and her friend Kathleen. We were just chatting away and drinking coffee when suddenly, I started to feel the presence of a female, a relative of Kathleen's. I looked at Kathleen and asked if I could say something. I really did not know Kathleen at this time and knew nothing about her family other than knowing her mom, but here was this female wanting to connect. Kathleen told me to go ahead.

"I told her there was a female who liked to fish and said she watches over Kathleen. The female said Kathleen's mom had regrets like maybe she could have stopped some of this soul's ways, and the soul wanted Kathleen to know no one could have stopped her. She showed me an image of her little girl in a living room spinning around and singing. The soul said she dances with her little girl.

"I started to ask Kathleen if her relative had a piercing, and before I could get the word piercing out, blood started dripping off the side of Kathleen's nose. Kathleen had not touched her nose since she was holding a cup of coffee. We ran to the bathroom and there was a small hole on the side of her nose that looked exactly like a nose piercing.

"Kathleen turned to me with big eyes and told me, 'Yes, she had a nose piercing in the exact same spot!'

"After we settled down from the nose bleed, Kathleen showed me a video of this relative's daughter—spinning and dancing in the living room."

Mary Grace (left), Aunt Kim's daughter with Kathleen

Chapter Thirteen

Spontaneous Readings

With Sara's gift, spontaneous readings can happen anywhere, anytime, nose bleed and even without a trigger. *(A trigger is someone or something associated with the deceased person or subject that causes an action; a trigger could be a picture, name, or object reminiscent of the deceased who is the focus of a request for a reading).* For example, consider Sara being able to tell me about La Nell, my daughter-in-law's deceased mother. Sara did not know me or my daughter-in-law, had seen no picture(s) of us, and did not even know my name; she had no connection with either of us, but she was able to do a reading and deliver a real message by way of a third party, ME. Now that's a gift!

In this chapter, you will hear about the many readings done with little or no information about, or connection to the spirit / soul sending the message(s). Many of these will be first hand experiences I witnessed. At this writing, I have known Sara for forty-three days; yet our bond is so strong that rather freaky things happen between us.

Case in point: Did you notice the very strange first sentence in this chapter such as the words "nose bleed" that did not fit? Two hours ago, I began writing this chapter by first jotting down some names and incidents I wanted to include in the chapter. Then I wrote the first line that would be my thesis statement for the chapter. Just as I got started, I got sidetracked with my second computer *(yes, I use two computers when I write)* and then went downstairs for a few minutes. When I got back to restart the chapter, I noticed something had been added to the unfinished thesis statement which made no sense at all. I know the paranormal exists, but NOT IN MY HOUSE PLEASE! Who typed those ridiculous two words on the end of my thesis statement? Here is the evidence.

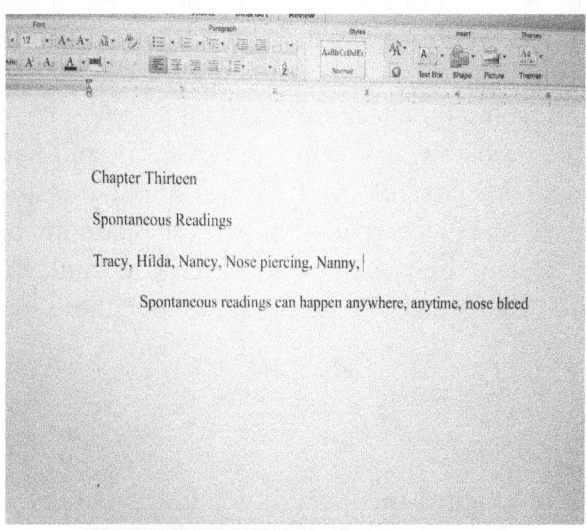

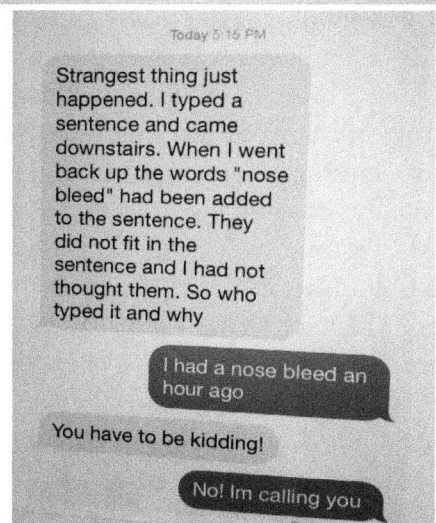

Exhibit A (The Unfinished Sentence);
Exhibit B (Text Messages with Sara)

Exhibit A is the first sentence of Chapter Thirteen. I had started this sentence and then got lost on my second computer and downstairs. As you can see, Exhibit A: **"Spontaneous readings can happen anywhere, anytime, nose bleed…"** does not make sense. Unnerved by the phantom hand who typed "nose bleed", I texted Sara and told her what happened. Exhibit B is her reply that further freaked me out! When she called seconds later, I answered by saying, "Why are you typing on my computer? LOL!"

By the way, I am in Cushman, Arkansas, and Sara is in her home in South Mississippi. And true, at about the time she had a nosebleed, a rare occurrence for Sara, a phantom hand typed "nose bleed" on my thesis statement. When you think about it, this "spontaneous" happening IS pertinent to my thesis statement. I think I'll keep it!

Brain Bleed

After the night I met Sara, it was inevitable I would write a book about her. I was totally mesmerized by her gift and how she used it for others. This would be my first nonfiction work, other than my mother's biography. However, I realize many will think the whole book IS fiction. You will have to take my word—or not—and the word of those whose messages are summarized in the book.

A few days after that night of filming, Sara came back to Yalobusha County, this time to start the interview process for the book. Sara's parents Randy and Denise came with her along with Sara's two children. They got to the cabin I had reserved for them late, but I was there within fifteen minutes with camcorder and tape recorder in hand.

From the first moment, they began telling Sara's story. I was so intrigued, many times I forgot to turn the tape recorder on. I tried to take notes but became so captivated listening, I finally gave up and prayed the tape recorder was doing its job for later transcribing.

Watching Sara and seeing her expression change when she got a message was a writer's dream. "Awe inspiring" is the best way to describe it.

In the middle of her mom telling about one of Sara's experiences as a child, Sara got a look in her eyes like she was somewhere else and started scribbling in her notebook. This would turn out to be a most important message and would cut her visit short. This was a vision of a future event but was only words. In her notes, Sara wrote " Brain, head, and bleed", but who was to be the

I left the cabin about 3:00 A.M., with plans for them to meet me at my house the next morning. Sara and I would take another trip to the cemetery where Betsy Bell is buried in hopes Sara could pick up more messages. One we both hoped would come to her was the "little lost boy", and we hoped he would tell us where he is buried, but that story will be covered in another chapter.

The next morning, Sara and her family arrived at my house. We sat drinking coffee around my husband's great grandparents' oak table and talked about what was next in our project. If furniture holds the energy of past owners, the voices should have been competing for wavelengths to Sara's brain since my cabin is full of primitive (*homemade*) antiques.

I wonder what would have happened if Sara had run her hand over the almost two hundred year old kitchen cupboard, or kitchen press as it was called, painted in old red buttermilk base paint by the maker. The heavy piece had belonged to a first cousin of Jefferson Davis, Father of the Confederacy (*I bought it from a Davis in Houston, Mississippi who had inherited it*). If that old cupboard could talk, maybe Sara could hear President Davis planning war strategies for the Confederate troops while he reached behind its doors to fetch sugar for his coffee; or perhaps, he would reach in it for a teacake made from an old family recipe.

Sara loved my log house, and as she walked through it, I had her take notice of any negative vibes. Since I tend to spend many hours sitting in graveyards at night, and other haunted locations, and talking to flashlights *(part of my ghost hunting routine)*, I am often uneasy thinking something may have followed me home. I have on occasion had mysterious things happen in my house. Fortunately, Sara did not pick up anything evil, but when she went upstairs, she picked up a "Nanny" and a "Pop" or "Papaw." She was unsure of the P word but said "Nanny" came through strong and clear.

That answered the question about furniture containing the energy of past owners since there is a rocking chair and a bed from each set of grandparents upstairs. The chair came from "Nanny" Clifton and Pop, and the bed came from "Nanny" Nelson and Papaw. Nanny "came through strong and clear" because there were two of them, and both Pop and Papaw shared their vibes as well. Amazing!

As we finished our coffee, Denise's cell phone rang, and I could see her face change from happy to anxious.

"We have to go home! Kim is in the hospital. They think she had an aneurism!"

Kim is Denise's youngest sister and she and Sara are very close. Our visit was cut short, but we did go by the cemetery for a quick fifteen-minute walk through.

Later that day, Sara called to tell me, it was not an aneurism; her "Kim had a brain bleed." Now we had the answer to Sara's hastily scribbled note "brain…head…bleed!"

Sara with Kim in hospital

Fortunately, Kim recovered and could not believe Sara had known about this the night before it happened. This time Sara knew the person well, but the message was spontaneous, without an actual trigger, and the message was about someone alive!

But what about the messages Sara gets from people she has never met and there seems to be no relationship or association of any kind. The following cases exhibit more "unsolicited" messages.

Hilda

A few days later, Sara and I would head to Adams, Tennessee to research for Part III. I invited my friend Hilda to come along, but Sara did not know her and only knew I had a friend coming with us.

The night before we left, Sara sent me a text message:

"Do you know a Lara and an Emily?"

I was amazed! These were Hilda's daughters, but how did Sara know this? She did not even know my friend's name. But the surprises did not stop there.

"Do you know anyone with a dog named Lady?" Sara's text asked.

"No. Why do you ask?" My curiosity was up.

"I'm getting a picture of a female calling a dog named Lady like, 'Here, Lady!' Then she makes sounds with her lips like kissy noises. 'Come here, Lady!' Then I hear a child's voice yell, 'I'm okay!'"

Sara caught me off guard this time. I did not know if one of Hilda's girls had a Lady in the family or not. I called Hilda and asked, "Does anyone in your family have a dog named Lady?"

After a long pause on the other end, Hilda said, "Emily does. Why do you ask?"

I proceeded to tell Hilda about the text message from Sara. Hilda was somewhat alarmed by it not knowing Sara, but she confirmed the entire message. In fact, Emily had gotten home from Jackson shortly before I received the text, had let Lady out and then called her back in with the kissy sounds. In the background, following a loud noise, Emily's younger daughter had yelled, "I'm okay!" This was something she had done since she was old enough to talk, and it was one of her favorite things to say. Her mom and dad knew if there was a crash, to wait for "I'm okay!" from their younger daughter.

Poor Hilda was so freaked out by Sara's vision, she almost didn't go the next morning! But it wasn't over yet.

Upon meeting Sara, Hilda's uneasiness changed quickly to intrigue and honest liking of Sara. Halfway into Tennessee, Hilda watched as Sara scribbled on her notebook "Ava…Princess…Cute Shoes."

Hilda asked to see Sara's notes and Sara said, "This just came to me. I have no idea why."

Hilda took over at this point and explained, "Ava is Emily's older daughter; she wants to be a princess at Disneyworld when she grows up, and she loves shoes!"

Sadie

Shortly after I got the text from Sara asking if I knew a Tracy, I got another text message asking if I knew a Sadie. Again I answered, "Yes."

"I see an older woman. She loves to bake and is an excellent cook. She also enjoys crafts and loves her God. She is holding her Bible."

I looked at the description of my mother's sister, but all I knew for sure was she baked the best orange cakes and desserts ever. When I was young, I loved going over to Sadie's house and getting to eat her wonderful baked goods. The rest I did not know, but I knew I could call her daughter and find out.

What was extremely interesting was my mother had been talking about how much she missed her two sisters and her brother Buddy, all of whom had passed away. She keeps family pictures, especially Buddy's, where she can see them from her bed.

I called my Aunt Sadie's daughter Teresa, and she confirmed everything Sara had said, even the parts I did not know.

"Mama loved to quilt and to crochet." Teresa began. "One Christmas, she gave all of us a quilt she had made. She also crocheted pillow covers. As for loving her God, yes, that was Mama, too. I remember one time she sold bonds for the church's building fund, and she was Training Union Director for years."

I could tell my cousin was enjoying talking about her mother. Sadie's children adored their mother and took her loss extremely hard. I told Teresa, Sadie wanted her family to know she was okay, which they already knew from her being a devout Christian. Teresa added one more remark before we ended our telephone conversation.

"My most prized possession is the Bible my mother gave me when I was a teenager. Mama loved her Bible and read it daily."

Sara had more knowledge about my Aunt Sadie than I did, something I am not proud to tell.

When I shared this experience with Mama, she did not question Sadie's appearance to Sara at all. After all, Mama talks to my dad and my Uncle Buddy every day. Both are deceased—Buddy recently but Daddy has been gone for years.

Following, you will find Sara's notes about Sadie, right under the notes about Tracy. I could never doubt Sara's connection with our God.

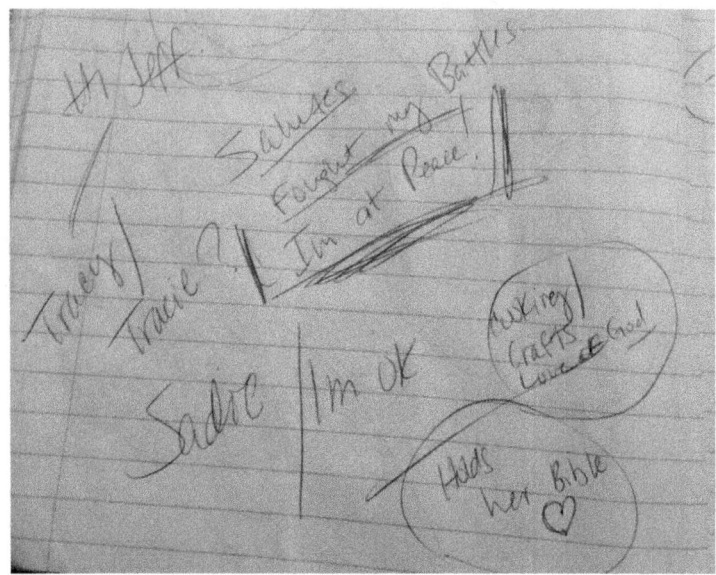

Sara's Notes about Sadie at the Bottom

Mildred, Sadie, & Jeannette
Sisters

Chapter Fourteen

Henry

On our second trip to Adams, Tennessee doing research for the book, we were fortunate to be able to stay in a cabin belonging to Robert (Bob) Bell, direct descendant of John Bell of the Bell Witch Legend *(Part III)*. Bob's daughter Anne Rickman and her husband Michael also came and stayed with us at the cabin. Anne and Michael are expecting a baby boy whose name will be Henry. Anne and Sara had become good friends through Facebook and through Bob who met Sara on the first trip to Adams. *(You will read more about Bob, Anne, and Michael and this trip in Part III).*

We had two nights and almost two days to revisit and to see some things missed on the first trip to the old legendary location. On our second day there, first full day, Tim Hensen, the museum curator, went with us to all the old historic sites as he did on our first trip. During one stop at a wonderful old tobacco barn, Anne waited on us in the car while we took pictures and walked around the barn. While sitting in the car, Anne's mind, of course, was on Henry. She began thinking of how Michael was saddened by his grandmother's death and how she would not be there for Henry's grand entry. Knowing of Sara's special gift and believing in Sara, Anne began talking in her mind, wishing for Michael's grandmother to connect with Sara and to deliver a message to her husband, something to console him.

We got back in the car and headed out again, and Sara looked at Anne and asked, "Do you have heart burn a lot?" Anne gave Sara a questioning look and Sara continued. I see this baby having a headful of hair, and indigestion is a good sign, or so I hear. But regardless, this baby is going to have a lot of hair!"

"You think so?" Anne asked smiling at Sara.

"Yep, a lot of hair." Sara confirmed. Sara had begun feeling strange, a precursor to receiving a message.

We stopped back by the cabin where Sara had seen a young girl in white on our first trip to Adams, and as Anne and Michael stood inside, Sara could see a haze around them, like a glow. With Anne being pregnant, Sara asked them to move to another spot, not wanting to take any chances of something questionable being that close to Henry.

We returned to the car and rode a while longer and Sara asked another question.

"Did either of you lose someone to cancer recently…an older female?"

"Yeah. My grandmother." Michael turned and looked at Anne who was sitting in the backseat between Sara and me.

"Well, that must be who this female soul is who just came to me. She needs for you to know she is okay. She knows you need to hear that." Michael's eyes became moist, while Anne's pretty face was etched in "Oh my goodness!"

"She also needs you to know you don't need to worry about her not holding Henry and rocking him like she used to rock you. I think you talk to your grandmother in your head and tell her you wish she could be here to rock Henry. Is that right, Michael?"

"Yeah. My grandmother always rocked me when I was a baby. I was really close to my grandmother."

Sara continued, knowing what she would tell him next would be a shock. "She wants you to know she already holds Henry and rocks him just like she did you. You don't have to worry about her missing that."

"Wow! Out of everyone in my family, it was my grandmother I wanted most to be able to rock my son. My grandmother always rocked me."

"And that's why she wants you to know she rocks him. She is getting Henry ready for ya'll. But now she wants to talk about her garden."

Michael started laughing and put his hand over his mouth. "Oh, my gosh! Her garden looks horrible. I just went over there and said I had to do something with it."

"You might want to do something because she's talking about her garden."

"She loved her garden." Michael smiled. "It does look awful though."

"Ooh! She's getting on to you, Michael. You better do something with that garden." Sara laughed and so did Michael, but you could see his eyes glisten.

We headed for the little café adjoining the museum, and when we got there, Sara began writing in her notebook again. Michael's grandmother had much on her mind and the messages kept coming.

"She says someone, other than you, too, got married recently. It was someone older than you."

"Yeah! Three weeks ago! Oh, my gosh!" This was shocking to Michael.

"She was there with them." Sara explained.

At this point, Anne confessed.

"I just want ya'll to know while I was sitting in the car waiting on you, I was kind of talking to Michael's grandmother hoping she would send a message through Sara to Michael since he misses her so much. I didn't really believe she would do it though."

As we left the café, Michael went to Sara and thanked her for delivering the messages from his grandmother. He told her it meant so much to him. His grandmother was more like a mom to him. Michael confirmed there was no way Sara could have known any of this, and he believed his grandmother spoke through Sara. Another case of total validation, and one that meant so much to Sara since she was friends with Anne and Michael and she had so much respect for Anne's father Bob Bell, Henry's soon to be grandfather. Henry will be Bob and Mary Lee Bell's first grandchild. This message made our travel to Adams very special and worth the long trip.

Chapter Fifteen

Nancy Jane

Another soul approached Sara from out of nowhere, totally spontaneous, but was so intriguing, unique, and emphatic in what she wanted, she deserves her own chapter. On Sara's way to the cemetery the night of the TV filming, an older woman appeared to Sara. The woman had gray hair and had her shoulders held back straight with excellent posture even though she was sitting in a wheelchair. Then the woman stood showing Sara she no longer needed the wheelchair and in a very articulate voice said, "I am Nancy, and I want to be known!"

Yes, this was bizarre, but Sara handles bizarre extremely well. To Sara, bizarre is normal; she's been experiencing it since she was three. Sara knew this was a soul with a message and figured she would run into someone at the filming who would know this very sophisticated lady. Sara did find someone that night whose mother's name was Nancy and assumed this was she, especially since that Nancy had to use a wheelchair right before she died of cancer. But the woman appeared to Sara again a day or so later, many times, in fact, and told Sara, "I am Nancy Jane and I want to be known!" Oops! Wrong Nancy the other night! Not good! This was a strong willed Nancy soul!

Sara said she could not see the background where Nancy Jane was located. She was visible but was surrounded by a mist, as many souls are when they make an appearance. Sara felt like the prim little woman was connected to the Bells some way.

I did not know who Nancy Jane was but I knew who would

know. I messaged Sharon Bell Hamilton and described the woman telling Sharon this lady first appeared to Sara on the road close to the cemetery on July 1st, the night of the TV filming.

"Yes, I know her." Sharon told me. Sharon is a great resource as is Mike Worsham the local historian, on the family ancestry of those who lived in the Long Branch community also known as Hatton. Sharon grew up in Arkansas but every summer, she visited her grandparents who lived here.

"Nancy Jane Wright Hughes married James Ransome Hughes, the son of Selah Thacker and Tarlton Hughes." Sharon began telling me the family background. "Nancy Jane's parents owned the property across the road from what later became Eliza and ZYX Bell's place. Nancy's home place became the Wright/Hughes Plantation. Nancy Jane was in a wheelchair and I have her picture. I got it from her great grandson Jim Turner. I can put it on my wall for you and Sara to see." Sharon added one more detail. "Nancy Jane was not related to the Bells but her daughter married Doc (as in Zadoc) Bell. The log cabin Nancy Jane lived in forms the center of the Wright/Hughes plantation house. They were neighbors to Eliza Jane and ZYX."

Bingo! The Wright/Hughes Plantation house is a large antebellum plantation home in a beautiful country setting in Yalobusha County, Mississippi. I pass it going to Long Branch Cemetery and have always admired the place. I told Sharon it was wonderful she was putting Nancy Jane's picture on Facebook. She "wants to be known!" I told Sharon.

"Nancy Jane is buried in the Hughes family plot across the road from my family in Long Branch Cemetery," Sharon added.

Now I knew we had the right person. Nancy Jane must have known something was going on at that cemetery that night in early July when the filming took place, and she was being left out of it. That's what happens when you are buried in the same cemetery with Betsy Bell Powell who many erroneously believe was "The Bell Witch."

As soon as I found Nancy Jane's picture on Sharon's wall, I showed it to Sara who began shrieking, "That's her! That's Nancy Jane!"

Not long after, my friends Hilda and Gayle joined me visiting Betsy Bell's grave as we have done many times. Also, the threesome from the Northern Lights adventure had not been together in months and needed to catch up. We took our chairs to the Hughes family section and sat with Nancy Jane for a while first. We got no reaction from flashlights or K-II meters, and I caught no voices on my camcorder but I talked to her just the same.

"Nancy Jane, you are not only on Facebook, (*She is an intelligent lady who obviously keeps up so I bet she knows what that is*) you are going to be in a book with your picture and your own chapter. Thank you, Nancy Jane, for getting Sara's attention. I wish I could have known you back in your day. I know you are happy, especially after pushing that wheelchair aside so many decades ago. Don't rest in peace, Nancy Jane! Kick up your heels!"

After a descent chat with Nancy Jane, we moved our chairs to visit Betsy Bell. Betsy has a bigger part in the book than Nancy Jane, but I bet Nancy Jane has some stories about Betsy she could add to Part III. I imagine they knew each other since they lived across the road from each other in Yalobusha County. If only tombstones could talk! Oh, wait—they can, as long as they have the right listeners!

Footnote to Nancy Jane: After writing this section, I sent it to Sharon just to make sure I got her information correct. Sharon called me and told me about a message she had received on Facebook from Nancy Jane's great grandson Jim Turner, the one who sent her Nancy Jane's picture. Jim is also a writer and is very proud of his family history and is quite knowledgeable about his ancestors. I emailed Jim and he sent me information on his great grandmother. Jim writes in a beautiful prose style of which I am sure Nancy Jane would approve. After reading the biography of Nancy Jane, I have become even more enamored with her. She is exactly as Sara envisioned her. More validation—this time from South Carolina! Here is Jim's description and a short biography of his great grandmother Nancy Jane Wright Hughes:

Dear Dr. Clifton,

Thank you for including Great Grandmother Nancy Jane in your book. She was a proud and honorable Southern Lady of whom I myself am quite proud. Nancy Jane was always a strong and independent woman with perfect poise and posture, dressed to the nines, even from her wheeled chair. I am not surprised she spoke boldly to the psychic wanting to be recognized.

Great Grandmother Nancy Jane Wright Hughes was a recognized equestrian before she was confined to her wheeled chair. She was injured while riding horseback, with a broken hip, I believe, and was confined to a wheeled chair for the remainder of her life. To my knowledge, Nancy Jane never complained.

During the War Between the States, she once defied a Union Captain, refusing to tell where the cured meats, livestock, etc., had been hidden, and the Captain, showing his irritation and thinking he would frighten this petite lady, jumped her with his horse as she sat in her wheelchair on the front lawn of Hatton. Nancy Jane, sitting straight and proper, never wavered nor blinked an eye, winning the hearts and respect of the Union regiment. Her paternal grandmother, after all, was a feisty Irish born lady, Nancy Agnes McMullen, born in Ireland in 1779.

Nancy Jane was an only child, some say spoiled, and as history has shown willful. Her position did not decree she must "marry well" or marry a man of considerable means. However, Nancy Jane's parents did not approve of her partiality, much less her engagement, to my Great Grandfather James Ransome Hughes, so in the middle of the night, she slipped out of an upstairs window and eloped to marry, without permission, in Oxford, Mississippi. Obviously she married for love, and this I admire as well.

The neighboring Hughes family was not wealthy. They were hard working farmers, known to be of good character, just not of the same social standing as the Wrights. After the marriage, the couple made their home at the Wright Plantation, which consisted of 1700 acres. Nancy Jane's father, George Washington Wright, acquired this land through the Chickasaw Pact and built the original log home on his first trip to Mississippi. The large Plantation home was built around the original log structure. Nancy Jane and her husband James raised their family, cared for their elderly parents, and in later years took their final rest here on the plantation.

Although prim, proper, educated and respected in the community, Nancy Jane, in essence, ran the plantation. Family and slaves alike loved and admired her. Black families at Hatton were not mistreated but were protected, well cared for, and stayed on after the war.

Thank you again, so much, for including Nancy Jane in your work. I hope you now have a better understanding of my willful, yet proper Great Grandmother.

Respectfully,
J Hughes (Jim) Turner

Nancy Jane Wright Hughes
1849-1915

Chapter Sixteen

The Thomas House

We walk slowly, each step deliberately placed as we listen for creaks in the old floor—creaks not caused by our shoes; for gunshots used in a man vs. man chase after a guest is caught in the bedroom with another man's wife; for the humming of a spirit child as she sings her baby doll to sleep. And we watch, ever vigilant, hoping to see shadows darting in and out of our peripheral vision; flashlights turning on and off, on and off, as spirits answer our probing and too personal questions; a ball rolling as if a ghostly hand has pushed it down a creepy hallway. And we hope to feel each spirit's presence with our senses—but not necessarily soliciting the pulling of our hair or touching of our bodies by phantom fingers lightly streaking down the back of a neck causing a double crop of chills. Such was our trip to the Thomas House.

Can a person HUNTED by the dead do an about face and HUNT the dead! After witnessing Sara's psychic abilities and her abilities as a messenger for the departed, I had to see what she could experience at my favorite haunted location, The Thomas House in Red Boiling Springs, Tennessee. Knowing Sara belongs to Mississippi Paranormal Investigations and has taken part in many investigations with Kate, her friend and founder of the group, I expected her to be open to the Thomas House. I already knew the spirits would come to her. They always do.

The Thomas House is a beautiful Victorian hotel built in 1890, by the Cloyd family. Originally, it functioned as a health resort with mineral springs running through and under the property and used as medicinal baths for healing. The Thomas House is home to many spirits who linger there or who are trapped for whatever reason. CNN named this hotel the second most haunted place in the U.S., and it lives up to its reputation. Several children spirits are among the "residents", and evidence of their existence has been captured by television paranormal shows such as Ghost Hunters, Paranormal State, and Ghost Adventures.

Since the Thomas House is only an hour and a half from Adams, Tennessee, I decided to take Sara there after our second research trip to Adams was finished. I also wanted her to meet the Coles, owners of the hotel since the early 1990's and my good friends.

As always, Sara asked no questions and sought no information about the location. The revelations Sara would get before ever setting eyes on the old hotel would be incredible and all spontaneous. But before going to the Thomas House, we would take one last opportunity to research the lands of John Bell of the Bell Witch Legend in Adams, Tennessee.

As we entered Springfield, Tennessee just a short distance from Adams, Sara held her head and asked me if I had anything for a headache. At one point, she thought she would be sick from the severe pain in her head. After she took the meds, the pain began to ease and she began scribbling in her notebook. Often, the first indication Sara is receiving messages is a headache, a stomachache, or chest pain, the pain or feelings being a counterpart to the suffering of the person who has passed, the one trying to reach her.

When Sara is able to explain her notes, she tells me this vision was a boy, twelve-years-old, who died in 2007 in a tragic accident; she told me the father's name as well as the boy's full name including his middle name. As we continued along the road, she added additional words and phrases: "mark on face, brown hair, baseball, drums, PJ's."

I told Sara I had no knowledge of this boy, or for whom the message was intended. Five minutes later, she said, "It's the Thomas House. I'm sure it's for the Thomas House."

I picked up my phone and dialed the hotel. Evelyn Cole answered and I gave her all of the information Sara had written in her notebook. Evelyn thought for a minute and said, "Yes, I remember that little boy's death and how tragic it was for his father and grandparents. They come to the Thomas House often and have been for years."

Once we had the names confirmed, I checked the Internet for the boy's obituary and other information. He was twelve years old and died in 2007, a tragic accident that took place in another state. I found pictures of the boy with a small mole or birthmark on his chin, photographed in a baseball suit, and in another picture holding pajamas he had received as a Christmas present. Drums were also mentioned as a gift. In the obituary, his grandparents, the friends of the Coles, were listed as extended family. (*I had met the grandparents, a really nice couple, a long time ago but had never met the boy or his father*). Once Sara's reading is validated, her headache eased—until other visions began to come to her; all visions were associated with the Thomas House, and Sara thought it could be to help her establish credibility with the Coles although some could be messages that needed to be delivered.

Next Sara received the name Trevor. "He had dark hair and was killed in an car wreck. I keep getting the year 2007 and don't think it was just for the other boy. Trevor was a young man but not a child. He could be a son of the owners."

I knew immediately this was the son of Darrell and Cherry Cole, owners of the hotel, and I was not surprised Trevor showed up. Darrell and Cherry are wonderful parents and grandparents, and they will never get over losing their son, one of twins, his twin brother being Tyler. Trevor's name soon showed up again with another soul.

Sara is introduced next to the most endearing little child spirit and a favorite of Thomas House visitors. She shows herself to Sara and asks, "Where's Trevor?" Darrell once told me Trevor loved children, and he would have enjoyed lavishing love and attention on his Tyler's children, two little boys and a girl.

Sara smiled talking about the little girl spirit who "twirls and dances and is barefoot."

"She loves getting into the makeup of female guests, and she has lipstick smeared all over her face as she dances and hums her little two-note song. She carries a baby doll and puts it to bed in a doll cradle with spindles on the side like a real baby crib."

"I can't get her name yet, but I will." Later, Sara said, "I think her name is Sarah, because she keeps pointing at me, but it's spelled different from my name."

I have caught Sarah humming those two notes as well as many other EVP's of her talking. The best EVP I caught of Sarah happened when I had children with me: my grandchildren Denver and Maggie and a former student Jada. Also with us was Pat Fitzhugh who is a regular at the Thomas House since he lives close by in Nashville. All children, including my grandchildren and the spirit children, love Pat.

As we sat in what is considered Sarah's room, I caught a Class A EVP of Sarah saying, "Pat comes to my house." Her soft little voice sometimes shows impatience with Darrell, one of her favorites, as she chides, "I'm right beside you" and "I'm mad at you…I'm princess!" Probably more EVP's of Sarah's voice have been recorded than any of the spirits at the Thomas House.

Sarah also likes to sit on the foot of guests' beds, especially if they are sleeping in Room 37, the most requested room and the one where she has most often appeared. Once she snuggled to my back like a small puppy seeking security or warmth.

On our way to the Thomas House, I looked over at Sara's notebook and noticed she had written 37, 37, 37…

"Would you like for me to tell you why you keep getting the number 37?" I asked Sara who let me know immediately that she did.

"It's the most active room at the Thomas House—and it's where we're staying."

Later, when we carried our bags into Room 37, Sara stopped and gasped.

"That's it! That's the doll crib where I saw her put the baby doll!"

Guests leave toys, especially dolls, for Sarah in room 37 and most of them lie resting, waiting for Sarah—in the doll cradle with spindles that looks like a real baby cradle. Sara had seen this in her vision exactly as it is.

Sara knew much through her psychic abilities before we even left Adams heading toward Red Boiling Springs and the Thomas House. She had envisioned a man in a Confederate uniform, a man who fell off a bridge and drowned, and a message Sarah kept giving her—something about really liking Diamonds music. That night we asked Cherry Cole who is a professional singer if Diamonds music meant anything to her. She said Diamonds was the name of a trio she once sang with, one that often performed at the Thomas House. Sara told her, "Well, it's Sarah's favorite music."

So much more was revealed at the Thomas House as we made our rounds through each room and hallway of the wonderful hotel accompanied by Darrell Cole and Cindy Smith, both members of Tennessee Ghost Hunters, but the vision that was the most shocking happened on the day just before we left on our trip to Red Boiling Springs, Tennessee.

I had risen early that morning and was sitting at the beautiful harvest table at the cabin where we were staying. I was working at my computer and drinking coffee when Sara came in. As she headed for the coffee pot, she stopped perfectly still and got in that stance I refer to as her point and began dramatizing what was happening. To Sara it was real, not a dramatization. Her hands began moving above her head as I watched spellbound.

"Oh, crap! He's underwater!" She began moving her hands over her head as if trying to surface. "He can't get out! He's drowning! The water is dark, but I see bubbles over me just like that little boy saw."

As Sara surfaced back to reality, she continued to express her horror at watching this.

"A little boy drowned there. I know what he felt! How awful!" Sara gave a little shake of her head and put her finger in her ear.

"Oh my gosh! I've got water in my ear! Look!" Sara showed me the shiny beads of water on her fingertip and I grabbed my phone and took a picture. I showed the picture to Anne and Michael who were staying at the cabin with us, but the next time I tried to show it to someone, the picture had disappeared from my photo collection.

Another vision Sara received, a story I had never heard, was concerning two little girls who drowned in Red Boiling Springs. When we got to the Thomas House, we asked Darrell about it and he confirmed this to be true. In 1969, there was a terrible flood and two sisters were swept away. Darrell could not remember the girls' names, but Sara had written down Renea and Jenni, later changing the second name to Jennifer. Darrell told us a small park in the town had been dedicated to the two little girls who drowned in the flood. Sara and I knew we would go there before leaving Red Boiling Springs.

As soon as Sara gave me the go ahead, I went to my computer and found information on the flood of 1969. Just as Sara said, the girls' names were Renea and Jennifer.

When Sara and I got to the Thomas House, I took her down what I call the creepy hall that is actually beautifully decorated in antiques like the rest of the hotel; it just tends to be very dimly lit—creepy, if you will. Sara immediately heard gunshots and arguing. Two men were fighting over a woman who was being accused of cheating by her husband. The argument resulted in the guest dying. I had heard this story many times but asked Darrell to tell it again to confirm it for Sara.

So what could be expected of someone like Sara who with her psychic abilities sees the dead, speaks to the dead, and delivers messages for the dead? Surely, she would be fearless—or would she? Could Sara be envisioned repeating that old line from *Ghost Busters*, "I ain't afraid of no ghosts!"

What if I told you, Sara IS afraid of haunted places? Many times that night in the Thomas House, my arm was grabbed as she sought motherly, or grandmotherly, security becoming an extension of my body. After we went to bed at 5:00 a.m., I watched as Sara jumped, jerking her knees up to her chin and rolling up like a blonde caterpillar in a cocoon. She said she felt "someone" sit on the foot of the bed. It was the opportunity I had been waiting for to do a little ribbing.

"It is just Sarah!" I told her, burying my laughter in my pillow.

I had watched in awe as this amazing young psychic walked

about the cemetery in the dark. One time, she even comforted me during the filming when I became fearful after an unexpected noise. When it happened, Sara put her hand on my shoulder and told me, "Don't be afraid; you are protected." Yet here she was in the Thomas House showing fear when the little girl spirit she enjoyed got a little bit too close.

But Sara's bravery would receive its ultimate test, not at the Thomas House, but when she opened herself up to receiving answers to the many questions remaining about the Bell Witch, the most popular ghost story in the United States.

Part III

The Bell Witch

Chapter Seventeen

The Bell Witch Legend

In the Foreword, I wrote I would attempt to answer the following questions when telling Sara's story: Can messages really be sent from beyond earthly life? Can these messages be communicated through human vessels put on earth by God *(not by the Devil)* for the purpose of comforting loved ones? Can the gift be used to answer age-old questions still haunting family members generations later?

In Parts one and two, the first two of these questions have been answered. Now it is up to each reader to decide if enough evidence has been presented to believe Sara is a vessel put on earth by God to deliver messages from departed souls. I believe there is sufficient evidence, but I suggest you open your minds and seek God's guidance before making your own decision.

One question remains to be answered: Can the gift be used to answer age-old questions still haunting family members generations later? In answering this question, the most famous ghost story, or paranormal mystery, in U.S. history will be studied. The Bell Witch Legend took place in middle Tennessee in the early 1800's and attracted hundreds of curious visitors, some from as far away as England, to the home of frontier settlers John and Lucy Bell. This legend includes the only murder in U.S. history attributed to a paranormal entity.

The "WAY", who I now know is my Heavenly Father, set the stage for providing answers to this haunting tale beginning three years ago when the first stepping stone was placed in my pathway. This path would also lead to Sara and the writing of this book.

Three years ago, my husband and I purchased a log cabin located in Yalobusha County, Mississippi. Our neighbor Lamar, knowing I was a ghost hunter and author, visited one evening and remarked, "You do know the Bell Witch is buried close to here, don't you?" I replied I did not know since I always assumed Betsy Bell was buried in Panola County where I had grown up.

Lamar convinced me it was a few miles down the road where Betsy Bell Powell of the Bell Witch Legend had lived and died and then her body interred in Long Branch Cemetery. I had heard of the Bell Witch all my life. The legend had been around for over a hundred years. Visiting the grave of the so-called Bell Witch had been a rite of passage for many teenagers in Panola County where it was assumed the witch grave was located. Climbing the Forestry Service fire tower was also a rite of passage. I climbed the tower as a teen, but I never visited the Bell Witch grave being extremely fearful of ghosts and such. What a contradiction my now senior years are to my long gone teenage years!

Who or what was the Bell Witch? None of my teenage friends nor I had a clue back in the 1960's, but it was thought going to her grave after dark was taboo; thus, many of my brave and rebellious friends had to go!

As a published author of paranormal mysteries, I have traveled thousands of miles all over the United States researching haunted locations. At each location, I ghost hunt using simple equipment such as flashlights, K-II meters, a camcorder, and a tape recorder. So what would I do now that I know the Bell Witch grave is close to my house? I began studying the legend to find out everything I possibly could about Betsy Bell, and I spent countless nights sitting around Betsy's grave with friends and fellow ghost hunters. As we sat huddled around Betsy talking to flashlights *(crazy but true)*, we caught many unidentified voices in the form of EVP's (Electronic Voice Phenomenon). As a result, I formed an addiction to and a strong camaraderie with Betsy.

All of this would lead up to the present, to Angel Leigh and answering age-old questions still lingering about the Bell Witch. To avoid lack of knowledge like what plagued me until three years ago, the story is being summarized up front before we get too deep into Sara's messages from these souls. No reader should be in the dark, no pun intended, while experiencing Betsy Bell's story.

Following is a brief summary of the Bell Witch Legend written by my good friend and fellow author, Ralph Gordon, who just happens to be married to a descendant of John Bell. Ralph plays another important role in the revelations about to be made in the book but this will be told a little later.

The Bell Witch

by

Ralph Gordon

Fabrications, half-truths, and even whole truths make up the ingredients of any good legend. But the Bell family of Tennessee and Mississippi will accept nothing less than the truth when it comes to the spirit that has haunted them since 1817. They called her Kate. Some folks believe the Bell Witch was a myth created by the imagination of the Bell family of Adams, Tennessee, but to many members of the Bell family, the witch exists today as it did in 1817, a real and living entity.

When one thinks of a witch, the usual stereotypes come to mind. But forget the image of the old hag with a long pointed nose, riding a broom, and dressed in a long black funeral dress and floppy black hat. According to those who believe in the Bell Witch, Kate is a spirit with one exception; she lacks physical incarnation, but most do believe the Bell Witch is a female.

There are as many versions of the origin of the Bell Witch as there are Bell Witch enthusiasts. Some of John Bell's descendants deny the existence of the witch altogether. They do not want their family legacy to be defined by a witch whether it is true or purely fabricated. Some Bell Witch researchers and historians now believe Native Americans placed the curse on any white man who happened to occupy the land in Tennessee, which means the curse was on the land and not the Bell family. If this is true, then the Bell family was simply in the wrong place at the wrong time.

One constant is that she (assuming the Bell Witch was female) first appeared to the family of John Bell near Adams, Tennessee, in 1817. However, there are some stories claiming that the Bell Witch saga began in North Carolina, but there is little or no documented proof of that. It is reported that John Bell first encountered the witch while plowing his field in Tennessee. He spotted a strange looking image of a creature that had the head of a rabbit and the body of a dog. The creature disappeared, but Bell believed it returned later when he heard strange sounds like someone beating on the side of his house followed by scratching at the door. When he went out to investigate, the sounds stopped, and whatever or whoever was making them disappeared into the darkness.

The sounds finally ceased as time went on, but the Bell family began to hear strange voices, barely above a whisper, not loud enough to understand until later when the witch gained power and became loud and often verbally abusive. For no known reason, the witch began to harass John Bell's twelve-year-old daughter Betsy. The harassment escalated into torment. The witch would slap her, pull her hair and cause her to have horrid nightmares. Kate's assault on Betsy actually left bruises on her face.

But the one who suffered the most was John Bell whose health began declining as soon as Kate appeared. In December 1820, John Bell died, supposedly poisoned by Kate. This is the only murder in U.S. history where a paranormal entity is considered the perpetrator.

One story of historical interest is of a visit by Andrew Jackson to the Bell home. John Bell's sons fought under Andrew Jackson at the Battle of New Orleans in 1814-15. One legend has it that Jackson was so intrigued by the stories he had heard that he decided to see for himself. In 1819, Jackson visited the Bell family in Adams. What he encountered defies imagination. As Jackson and his entourage approached the Bell farm, horses pulling the wagons froze in their tracks. They either could not, or would not pull the wagon any closer no matter what amount of coaxing the drivers applied. When Jackson shouted it must be the Bell Witch spooking the horses, a female voice rang out from the woods telling Jackson they could proceed and would meet again in the evening.

Later that evening, as legend has it, Jackson did meet with

the invisible witch. One of Jackson's men claimed he could tame the witch but was surprised when from out of nowhere, he felt a strong kick to his backside. His men were so terrified they begged Jackson to leave immediately, but Jackson was determined to learn what was causing the aberrations and stayed the night, not leaving for Nashville until the next morning.

Note: There is some doubt that Jackson visited the Bell farm in 1819. At that time he was heavily involved in constructing a new road from Nashville to New Orleans. Jackson personally oversaw the day-to-day operations of the construction. Many believe Jackson would not have made a special trip to Adams, which is about fifty miles northwest of Nashville, the opposite direction from where he was working on the New Orleans corridor.

Two of John Bell's children later moved their families to Panola and Yalobusha Counties in Mississippi to escape the curse of the witch. Betsy, herself, moved to Yalobusha County in her elder years after her last son's death to live with her daughter Eliza Jane and her husband ZYX Bell.

There is much controversy whether or not the Bell Witch followed the family members Jesse and Esther as they moved to Mississippi. But many believe Betsy Bell continued to be harassed by the witch to some degree, and her nightmares persisted in her new Mississippi home. In fact, she was so terrified she refused to be alone in the house for fear of the witch. She always slept facing the wall and would not sleep alone, requiring a grandchild to sleep with her on the outside of the bed. Betsy Bell died in 1888 at the age of eighty-two and is buried in Yalobusha County, Mississippi.

Kate has vowed to return. When will that be and who will be her next mark?

Ralph Gordon

Many theories of the *true* story of the Bell Witch abound—so many that a writer can get bogged down in trying to decide which theory seems the most credible. I have always said the only way we will know the truth is if the real characters in this legend speak to us from the grave. Enter Angel Leigh (Sara)!

On the night of July 1, 2015, I met Sara, the one person who could bring to light what really happened in those four fateful years (1817-1821) in Tennessee. How would she be able to do this? By receiving messages from the real life *(though now passed)* characters, the souls who played in the original, true version of the Bell Witch Legend.

Chapter Eighteen

Long Branch Cemetery

In the almost two hundred years since the entity who called itself Kate made its appearance on the John Bell farm in Adams, Tennessee, historians, paranormal experts, movie producers, and writers have developed many different theories in an attempt to answer the question: What was Kate? A ghost? A witch? A poltergeist? An angel? A demon? Why did it choose John Bell's family to torment? Was the Bell family, indeed, cursed?

With so much time and energy already devoted to researching the Bell Witch, I have no desire nor need to replicate. Many scholarly works exist, not the least of which is *The Bell Witch: The Full Account* by my friend Pat Fitzhugh who has researched the legend for over twenty years. Pat's website www.bellwitch.org has a massive amount of information and resources.

Another book I have studied extensively is *The Black Patch Bells: The Story of John & Lucy Bell* by another good friend Tim Hensen, the curator of the museum in Adams, Tennessee, who also researched for over twenty years. Tim is not a Bell descendant but is a trusted friend of the Bells from Robertson County. Tim, like me, is intrigued by the legend. Unlike me, he has a tremendous wealth of knowledge on the real characters and can quote names, dates, places, and events as if he had been there in the early 1800's. Tim acted as our tour guide on our two trips to Adams, taking us to all the places of significance such as original home sites and old cemeteries where the legend began.

An Authenticated History of the Famous Bell Witch by M.V. Ingram (1894) was, supposedly, based on the diary of Richard Williams Bell, second youngest child of John and Lucy Bell. Richard Williams Bell's account remains the closest document to a primary source since Williams was an eyewitness even though he was very young when Kate tormented his family. The only thing keeping it from being a true primary source is he wrote it many years after the fact. Still, this account makes the legend more history than myth. Williams was six years of age when the entity came to his home and ten when it left. His recollections, written in 1846, more than two decades after Kate left, provided the background and main source of information for Ingram's book. Richard Williams Bell's manuscript, *Our Family's Trouble*, consists not only of his memoirs of those troubling years but also the reminiscences of other members of the Bell family including Betsy. But Williams and his siblings were all bound by an agreement to publish nothing about the witch's stay at the Bell farm until the last member of the John and Lucy Bell family had died. Unfortunately, the original journal by Richard Williams Bell has never been found. Now that would be a primary source! In the meantime, I just accept the Ingram account and wait for Williams Bell's journal to mysteriously show up!

The Bell Witch: A Mysterious Spirit by Charles Bailey Bell, MD, is based on information handed down from the author's father Dr. J.T. Bell, son of John Bell, Jr., who was the second oldest child of John and Lucy Bell. This book tells the same story as the Ingram book but is much easier to read since it was not written in the prose style that Ingram loved and used.

Even with so many books and articles written and so many movies and television programs produced, the Bell Witch Legend still remains a mystery. Did the entity really exist? Too many experiences were witnessed during the four years of the spirit's presence for it not to have been real including hundreds of people who traipsed through the Bell farm hoping to experience this ghostly phenomenon.

I am a mere ghost hunter and author of seven published novels, all fiction. So what information could I possibly add to the Bell Witch Legend? The answer is I can add empathy and the desire to understand Betsy Bell, woman to woman.

Betsy once stated that she had a happy life but doesn't a happy life include a feeling of security? How could one who had suffered as much as Betsy, live a happy life? She was physically tormented for at least three years as an adolescent; broke her engagement with the love of her life Joshua Gardner because of fear of retaliation from the witch; outlived all but two of her eight children; lost her husband Richard Powell after twenty-four years of marriage, his death following many years spent as an invalid; experienced poverty and homelessness and was forced to move to Mississippi to live with her daughter Eliza Jane in her last years; suffered in her elderly years from obesity and poor health; and lived in a constant state of fear up until the day she died at eight-two.

I admit to being more than intrigued with Betsy Bell's story; I am addicted! With the first visit to Betsy's grave in September 2012, I felt she had many hidden secrets that needed to be told. Okay, I'll admit it! I sometimes feel Betsy is attempting to speak to me from the grave even though the voices I catch at her grave rarely include female voices.

Do I believe Betsy has passed on to receive her heavenly rewards? Absolutely! Betsy Bell was a Christian lady who suffered tremendously in her life. Her God, the same one who is my God, would never allow her more torture in the afterlife than what she had to endure on earth. What happened on those many trips to Betsy's grave that made me feel such amity with Betsy, and how does this all relate to Angel Leigh?

I will begin at the beginning at Long Branch Cemetery.

My first visit to Betsy's grave was after dark September 7, 2012. My neighbors went with me to locate the cemetery, a trick in itself, and then to search for Betsy's tombstone hidden in waist-high grass. I was surprised at the newness of her tombstone but later found out this one had replaced the original that was in terrible shape. A member of the Bell family had removed the tombstone in order to preserve what was left of it. The original now resides in the family member's garage.

Seeing the vandalism in the wonderful old cemetery depressed me and made me see the necessity for saving Betsy's original tombstone. So many vestiges of Mississippi's pioneer history lie face down or in cracked or broken pieces in that historic cemetery. The tombstones of Eliza Jane and ZYX (Zadoc Yelvington Xeres) Bell also lie on the ground rather than stand on the pedestals where they originally watched over their young children's graves. Carved in Betsy's headstone is a beautiful reading even though it has a few grammatical errors:

Tombstones of Betsy Bell Powell
A LOVE ONE HAVE GONE FROM CIRCLE
WE SHALL MEET HER NO MORE
SHE HAS GONE TO HER HOME IN HEAVEN
AND ALL HER AFFLICTIONS ARE OVER

Since that first night in 2012, I have lost count of the times I, with friends, have sat in the old dark cemetery, illuminated only by moonlight parting the branches of giant ancient oak trees; historical tombstones, the ones still standing, casting shadows around us while whippoorwills and owls perform background music for the perfect ghostly setting.

With each visit we listen for a female voice hoping Betsy will connect with us, but all we catch are many different adult male voices. Perhaps, we are hearing the slow, melodic drawl of a lingering Rebel soldier not wanting us to leave as he follows us to our car begging *What about me?* Or maybe the different male voices we catch are the sharp tongued, fast oratory of Yankee soldiers who do not speak southern, all possibly fallen during the local battles at Water Valley and Coffeeville: *Turn the light on! Talk to me! I don't know!*

All voices captured are intelligent and react to what we are saying or questions we are asking. On two occasions, we catch female voices. The first time is at the slave graves located in the woods and not directly on the cemetery grounds. Meredith, my oldest granddaughter, spoke specifically to Cass, one of the slaves supposedly buried there, "Cass, are you here?" A high pitched reply was recorded, "Uh huh!"

On another occasion when Pat Fitzhugh was with us at Betsy's grave, a strange set of bright eyes appeared over Betsy's tombstone as the flashlight went crazy. As this happened, I recorded a chorus of female voices almost like a chant saying, "Go back to the light!"

One night a frightened little boy spirit hovered beside us as if seeking refuge with this group of older grandmas. Right into my camcorder, he cried, "He dudn't like me! Oh!" The boy's voice, caught in the first five minutes after arriving at the cemetery, has haunted me for three years. Why is this little boy still here, and why is he not in heaven where I believe all children go upon dying? Does he have a connection with Betsy Bell, or does he just happen to be buried in the same cemetery with her and her family? The answers, or some of them, would come as a result of a chain of events.

On June 19, 2015, two weeks before I met Sara that first night for the TV show filming, I was invited to Long Branch Cemetery by my friend Sharon (Bell) Hamilton—yes, another descendant of the Bell family, this one of the Mississippi Bells. Sharon is the keeper of the family records for the Mississippi Bells and is working on a book that will serve as a guide to the John Bell family and will include deeds, estates, and records of many legal documents. It will also be a genealogy of the family in Robertson County, Tennessee, with special emphasis on the Bell children who moved to Yalobusha and Panola Counties in Mississippi.

Long Branch Cemetery has dozens of unmarked graves, and Sharon, with the help of professional dowser and author Ralph Gordon set out to find and mark these graves that Saturday. Two other Bell family members were part of the group, Barbara and Pat. Pat is Ralph's wife, and Pat, Ralph, and I developed a friendship that day. The next weekend, Pat brought me my own set of dowsing rods made by Ralph. Two other non-Bells, Mike Worsham, the local historian for Yalobusha County, and Nell Crocker whose family acts as caretakers of the cemetery, were keenly interested in the process and the findings. I thought to myself upon arriving at the cemetery, the very presence of three direct descendants of John and Lucy Bell might provide the trigger for some big surprises!

I showed up at the cemetery with my trusty camcorder and tripod ready for action, and Ralph did not disappoint me. Not only did he find many unmarked graves, he searched for child size, shallow graves at my request. I believed my "little boy lost" had been the victim of a horrible crime and his body probably disposed of quickly in a shallow grave.

Near the edge of the woods, just behind Eliza Jane's family tombstones, two unmarked graves were found—child's graves—and shallow. My heart leapt into my throat! But what could I do to find out if my little boy was in one of these graves? Could I get a court order to exhume an unidentified body, what was left of it, not knowing if it had been there ten years or one hundred years and not knowing for sure if any crime had been committed? Maybe I would just carry a shovel the next time I came here—for a little digging under the moonlight as the whippoorwills and owls serenade and the mosquitoes dive bomb in protest!

My answer would not be forthcoming this trip, but in the meantime, my job was to download footage taken that day as I watched Ralph dowse for graves. Sharon invited me to go to the Bell family reunion the next day. In order to thank her, I prepared a DVD showing the unmarked grave project from the day before. I also posted it to YouTube for other family members to see.

One thing many people do not know is paranormal activity does not only happen at night. This daytime footage delivered some of the best EVP's I have ever caught and also gave me the biggest cold chills ever with the exception of "He didn't like me! Oh!" And after I published the finished product on YouTube and made it public on Facebook the next day, I got another surprise jolt—all the way from North Carolina!

Chapter Nineteen

Little Boys Lost

Dowsing or Divining

Ralph moves to the edge of the woods still searching and his dowsing rods cross. I watch and wait hoping it is my little boy.

"This is a child's grave," Ralph says. "About three to four feet deep." Ralph had explained earlier he couldn't tell the gender of a child's body unless it is a female who has reached puberty.

He finds a shallow grave of a small child but will it be my little boy? After Sharon flags the spot, I begin talking, hoping for a response in the form of a little voice. If it isn't heard with our ears in the form of a disembodied voice, then perhaps it will be heard as an EVP later.

"Little boy who is lost, if you turn the flashlight on, I'll know it's you, or if you say something to me, I can hear you in here *(I point to the camcorder)*. Come beside me and say it where I can hear you."

"Find me!" A faint little voice is caught on the camcorder, but I won't hear it until I download the footage and amplify his sweet voice.

"Tell him nobody here will hurt him." Pat suggests. "Tell him we are all his friends."

"Little Boy!" I begin. "We want to help you pass on. All these people here are your friends. They want you to be able to pass on and go to Jesus, and we think we have to find where you are. If we can find you, then we can figure out what happened to you."

"This is me! I'm right here!" The little boy speaks louder in an excited, singsong voice. He wants to be found!

As I listen to the footage when I get home, tears stream down my face. We have found him! Or at least we have found a little boy! Is this what it takes for a child who is lost to pass on and be with Jesus? Is Jesus leading us as Christians to put forth the effort to find these little souls who somehow have become trapped between worlds? Maybe we will never know. The voice sounds younger than my frantic little boy of three years ago, but I know it is a little boy.

As I continue listening to footage, I notice more voices coming through in the same area where the little boy is found, but these are not happy voices. They are male adult bass voices chanting in a minor chord, "Fol-low me…me! Fol-low me…me!"

They repeat the same chant over and over. I add it to the iMovie I'm producing with some concern; the chant sounds creepy and somewhat demonic. Cold shivers circulate through my body! I wonder if the ones behind these voices are the ones keeping this little boy, and possibly others, from passing on. I want to turn it off, but I know I need to add it to the iMovie. After I finish, I add a warning about the chants.

The next day, I attend my first ever Bell family reunion. I feel honored to be part of this group although I realize many of them do not want to discuss the Bell Witch. What would it be like to be identified by a spirit who tortured children as well as adults and killed the head of the family? Still, I find the legend intriguing, and many of the Bell family members do as well, especially the younger ones. Others do not want to think of their family as being cursed and I can fully understand that logic.

The Bell family members seem interested in the DVD. They request to hear it more than once wanting to see if they can decipher the voices they are hearing. Some comments are made and a few questions are asked. I put the iMovie on YouTube so they can watch it again—or not.

That night, I get a message from Sharon telling me a woman named Brenda Abernathy who is an old high school friend of hers who grew up in Water Valley, will be calling me shortly—from North Carolina. Sharon tells me Brenda called and expressed how much she enjoyed the YouTube. Some of Brenda's deceased husband's family are buried in that cemetery, so Sharon knew Brenda would find it interesting and sent her the link. The remark from Brenda that shocked Sharon was when Brenda said she loved the part where the little blonde boy showed up by the woods.

"What little blonde boy?" Sharon asked.

"The one at the edge of the woods." Brenda explained. "He had the sweetest little face and had on some kind of old fashioned top with a white collar. He looked right at me with his little round face. Such a pretty little boy!"

"You better call Sue!" Sharon told Brenda and looked for my number. Then Sharon shot me a message so I would expect a call from Brenda.

Brenda is an absolute joy, and another friendship was formed even though we have never met in person. Brenda saw so much in the YouTube not visible to me or any one else. It seems Brenda has psychic abilities of her own.

"The little boy looked to be about three years old and had blonde hair with his bangs cut straight across like little boy haircuts back in the 1800's or early 1900's." Brenda's voice smiled as she described what she saw. The little boy would be unforgettable to her.

"It looked as if we were in real time as I looked at him and he looked at me. He kept his eyes on me, and his little round face lit into this big smile, and I think he clapped his hands at first but I'm not sure. I was mesmerized by what I was seeing, but I thought everyone else could see him, too. He was such a joyous little thing. His collar was white, but it looked like he had something black wrapped around and under the collar. I could not see below his shoulders but he moved like a little boy, too."

Brenda went on to tell me there was a body wrapped in a white cloth almost mummy looking, and it was suspended above the graves, floating beside the little boy. We discussed the possibility of it being his mother since Ralph did find a small adult female buried in another unmarked grave at an angle to the child's grave. Also in the picture, Brenda saw skeletons in rows. Neither Brenda nor I had an explanation for that.

While writing Part III, I checked in with Brenda to see if she had seen the little boy anymore when watching the movie.

"I have looked back many times but I no longer see him. We only connected that one time, but he gave me joy just looking at his precious smiling face."

That night when Sara arrived at the cemetery for the filming, she saw a little boy run across the road in front of the car in which she was riding. He stopped and peeked at her from behind a tree. Sara described him as a little boy of about seven with knee socks and short pants. "He was dressed like maybe the early 1900's, but I'm not sure." Sara explained.

The next time I saw Sara, I played the footage where the little boy says, "He dudn't like me! Oh!" I told her it sounded like he was frightened of someone as if he were being chased.

Sara gave me a different explanation.

"I see him lying in a pool of sweat. He is suffering from a fever and his mother places a cold wet cloth over his forehead. He died of a fever, maybe yellow fever, and was buried hurriedly in an unmarked grave." Sara summarized her vision for me. "He roams the cemetery, hides, and peeks from behind trees as he watches when people come to the cemetery. The boy is trapped and cannot pass on. We have to find his grave and give him a proper burial, a funeral service. Then he can cross over."

"But he sounds so frightened!" I explain the uneasiness I have endured since that night when I first heard his voice on the downloaded footage from my camcorder. "He sounds like he's running from someone who is trying to hurt him when he cries 'Oh!'"

"He is just frightened and very shy and wants to be with his family." Sara smiles giving me the relief I have needed all these years. "He wants to cross over. He cried out because he tripped when he was running to keep up with you. No one is trying to hurt him."

I still do not understand why the little boy has not gone to heaven, but I feel better knowing he is not being chased by some demon. Now I am determined to find his unmarked grave and arrange a proper burial securing his place with Jesus—something long overdue. And I think I know where to start.

After I met Sara and she explained about the seven year old boy who died of the fever, I let her listen to the YouTube where the younger boy speaks. I did not tell her what Brenda had seen.

"This little boy is about three. He is not the same as the other one. This little boy has passed on. He has crossed over into heaven."

As Sara ends, I smile. Maybe our finding his grave allowed him to pass on.

"This is me!" Perhaps now when the boy says these words, he will be looking up— "I'm right here" at the feet of Jesus.

To watch the video of dowsing and finding this lost boy, follow this link.

YouTube: https://youtu.be/HB6_YLal9bg

On our second visit to the cemetery when Sara and I only had a few minutes, her visit cut short by her Aunt Kim's brain bleed, Sara felt she might have found the grave of our seven-year-old boy.

"I think this could be his grave here, but I'm not sure." Sara walks over the spot where Ralph found an unmarked grave. As she looked down at the pink flags left by Ralph, she said, "I'm getting a J."

That night, as I went over footage at the cemetery, our short second trip, a male voice was heard right behind Sara's when she says she gets a J initial.

"This one's Jimmy. This…one's…Jimmy." The new hidden voice repeats his message succinctly. This male voice was not frightening.

Chapter Twenty

Souls of the Bell Witch Legend

The filming day finally arrived, and I made my way to the cemetery never expecting this shoot to change my life in such a thrilling way. Sara established her credibility with me through La Nell's message as we stood at Betsy's grave. Later, while the production and camera crew were taking a break, Sara and I returned to Betsy's grave and the two of us began talking to Betsy—or whoever.

The cemetery was extremely active on the night of the shooting with many EVP's caught by Sara and me during our thirteen-minute private session at Betsy's grave and by the camera crew. Sara was in tune with the souls, and I wish I could tell you what all was caught that night, but this would violate the confidentiality agreement I signed with the production company.

Sara heard the same voices a week later, but they were much more specific in what they were trying to tell Sara. The same would be true throughout the next two months to other sites as far away as Tennessee. The souls were not going to pass up the opportunity to have their messages delivered by a trustworthy messenger like Sara.

On our second short trip to Betsy's grave on July 9, Sara heard what she assumed to be a female voice telling her "Chloe did it", but the voice did not say what Chloe did. Sara also saw a woman hanging in a tree, but before she could get a good description of her, Sara's focus was redirected to a slave woman who showed herself behind a fenced-in family plot. The slave woman proved to be Chloe, the mother of Dean and the favorite slave of Lucy Bell. Chloe, with her son Dean, had been a wedding present to Lucy from her father in North Carolina, and Chloe and Dean moved with Lucy and her family to Tennessee in 1804.

Chloe mentioned something about her baby, and Sara caught on that this was a grown man Chloe was calling her baby, her son Dean. I did not catch Chloe on my camcorder. She showed herself to Sara only and she spoke to Sara only.

Sara told me Betsy had peacefully crossed over. She assured me Betsy can come back and forth for brief visits but won't allow herself to be trapped on this side. Perhaps female angels travel with Betsy when she comes back reminding her when it is time to "Go back to the light!" if she tarries too long at the graves of her family.

"Betsy is a strong soul, very strong." Sara was emphatic about this.

Sara's words gave me great comfort. This is something I have worried about when using flashlights to try to communicate with Betsy, or any soul, for that matter. As someone recently put it, "Flashlights are no different from Ouija Boards if you use them to summon the dead." This made me look at the way I use these in a whole new light. But when Sara is with me, I don't need flashlights, tape recorders, or K-II meters. Sara is a live piece of equipment, the best, and she doesn't call anyone forth. They come to her of their own free will. I get the messages and information firsthand when Sara gets it, and it is immediate with no waiting for download and review.

Even though it was daylight, Sara remained in the dark when it came to the Bell Witch. She purposely did not look for information on the legend and had no idea what it was. This is the way Sara works.

The legend tends to belong to Tennessee first and Mississippi second. The story of the witch harassing the Bell family of John and Lucy Bell took place in Robertson County, Tennessee, from 1817 to 1821. The legend was carried to north Mississippi when Jesse and Esther, two of the Bell children, moved their families to Panola and Yalobusha Counties in the late 1830's. Sara knew none of this, and neither did she know the stories behind Chloe, Betsy, Dean, or any of the names she heard at Long Branch Cemetery. It would take other trips to this cemetery and trips to Adams, Tennessee for Sara to really connect with Betsy and Chloe and to gain their stories surrounding the Bell Witch.

We only had a few minutes at the cemetery, but one quick image would provide the most important piece of the puzzle. A new telling of the Bell Witch legend began to surface.

Chapter Twenty-One

The Phantom Woman

Betsy walked out one evening soon after this with the children among the big forest trees near the house and saw something which she described as a pretty little girl dressed in green, swinging to a limb of a tall oak tree.

(*An Authenticated History of the Famous Bell Witch* by M.V. Ingram)

On July 21st, I was going through photos on my phone and came across the pictures I had taken at the cemetery showing the flagged, unmarked graves that had been dowsed by Ralph Gordon several weeks prior. I felt guilty when I realized I had never sent these pictures to Sharon who had requested them. Quickly, I sent them off to Sharon and then began looking at each picture.

As I scanned one picture, I noticed something standing near a tree in the back portion of the cemetery from where I was shooting. Upon close scrutiny, I realized it was the figure of a person dressed in a long dark dress or cloak. Immediately, I began enlarging it until the phantom figure came into clear view.

"It's a man in a dark cloak!" I said aloud after close scrutiny. The phantom figure looked very dark and foreboding. My thoughts traveled back to the male chant I had heard while Ralph was dowsing. On August 8th, as I headed up I-40 with Sara and my friend Hilda on our way to Adams, Tennessee, I pulled out the pictures I had printed off before leaving the house, one actual size and the other enlarged.

the night in the Bell home only to be awakened by strange noises followed by their bed covers being jerked off. The entity gave its loud, sardonic laugh, frightening Mr. and Mrs. Johnston out of their wits, and then it turned upon Betsy hitting her with fierce blows about her face. Nothing her parents or James Johnston attempted could stop the spirit's attack on the young girl. At Johnston's suggestion, John Bell opened up his house to others hoping someone could get to the bottom of this thing wreaking havoc on his family, especially his young daughter Elizabeth who the entity called Betsy.

After leaving the cemetery, Tim led us down by the stream where Betsy Bell often played with friends, Theny Thorne, adopted daughter of James Johnston, and Alex Gooch, Rebecca Porter, and others.

As we passed behind the old weathered barn and stacks of hay, Sara stopped and cocked her ear to one side.

"Listen! Do you hear it?"

Of course we heard nothing, but Hilda and I watched with interest as Sara began scribbling in her notebook.

"John!" Sara mocked the female voice she could hear calling John Bell. Immediately following, Sara heard Betsy calling in a totally separate conversation. "Daddy! I'm over here, Daddy!" Sara dramatized what she was hearing. Betsy was obviously answering her father John as he called for her, but Sara did not hear the father calling.

As we walked beside the creek, Sara stopped, and with fingertips rubbing together as they always do when she is receiving messages and visions from beyond, Sara began writing notes fast in the composition book she carried.

"I see a woman in a dark dress, hanging from a big oak tree. Betsy and a boy, maybe her brother, are walking toward the woman. They stop when they see her in the distance, but they are curious so they continue toward her. When they see it's a woman hanging by a rope, they turn and run. They stop a few feet away and look back. The woman has disappeared."

Sara does not know the story appeared in the original books written on the Bell Witch. Nor does she know Betsy saw a woman later, as Charles Bailey Bell wrote, "strolling about the orchard." Sara told how Betsy spoke to the woman a second time when she saw her, but this time she did not get an answer. The woman disappeared again. Was it the same woman? One important phrase in Sara's notes must be stressed above everything. The words "No Evil" became Sara's feelings toward the phantom woman and the girl in white. But both are not finished appearing to Sara in real time.

As we left the cemetery and proceeded down the highway, not far from the Johnston Cemetery Sara yelled, "Stop!" We had just crossed a bridge over the same creek, down from where Sara had seen the vision of the woman hanging.

"I just saw a young boy walking down the creek under the bridge. He had on brown pants and a cap."

Sara could not identify the boy, but she knew from the start the girl in the white dress was connected to the woman seen hanging in the oak tree in Tennessee—the same woman seen by Sara in Long Branch Cemetery in Yalobusha County, Mississippi.

In a later conversation with Sara, she told me, "I actually see the girl in white everywhere I go. The first time I saw her was in my home in south Mississippi right after I had been called and asked if I would be in the filming for the TV show on the Bell Witch. I had no idea who the girl was, or who she was connected to at that time. She follows me for a reason, and I feel we will know eventually when the time is right. She never speaks in sentences. The most I have gotten from her has been, 'Hi.'"

So where is the girl now and what is her story? More information would come from two different directions—North Carolina and the cabin belonging to Bob Bell in Cedar Hill, Tennessee, where we would stay on our second visit to Adams.

Chapter Twenty-Two

Girl With a Rope

After the first trip to Adams and one more trip to Long Branch Cemetery in Mississippi, Sara's mind, like her notebooks, was overflowing. Realizing I was pushing Sara to make sense of all of these visions, I backed off and began concentrating on writing Sara's life story, the first two parts of the book and the most important. If I cannot portray this blessed young woman establishing the credibility she deserves, then I have missed my calling as a writer and as a Christian. I have known Sara for almost two months at this writing and Sara and I believe we met for a reason.

I was meant to write Sara's story!

I was meant to be the one to tell Betsy's story as seen through Sara's eyes!

With God's help, I will make readers believe!

Shortly after the trip to Adams, I drove to south Mississippi with my fourteen-year-old granddaughter Maggie who was along to help entertain Sara's two children while Sara and I worked on the book. We spent one day with Sara driving me around showing me everywhere she had received a vision or had a significant occurrence in the early part of her life: from the schoolyard where the grim reaper type man in a dark long cloak stood watching her at lunch, to the homestead where she tried to outrun the shadows always chasing her; from the discount store where her son Randyn pointed to the old man smoking cigars, to the bridge by the creek where "the bird people live;" But the one place Sara never dreamed of being able to show me was the once home of the "Stinky Poo Poo Man."

As we passed by the house she had lived in when she was three, Sara saw a woman standing in the yard. Sara wanted to stop and talk to the woman in hopes we could go inside but did not know what to say. I told her to go back, pull in the driveway, and tell the woman she had once lived in the house and the rest would come to her. Sara turned around, did just as I suggested and found the woman to be extremely nice and friendly. To our surprise, she invited us in to see the changes she and her husband had made in the house.

Sara is honest to a fault and told the lady immediately why the house was so important to her. When she finished telling about the smelly old soul who lingered in the house when she was little, the woman surprised Sara by telling her about her son being frightened by an old woman spirit he said kept coming out of the closet in his room when he was a teenager. The owners had upgraded the house and made it a beautiful, comfortable home, the kind that made you want to curl up in a chair and read a good book—or write one, and it was no longer creepy.

While we were inside the house, Sara called her mother to tell her she was actually inside the house. Sara was excited on the phone and began her conversation with, "Mom, guess where I am?" She then began telling Denise how it came about, and Denise, too, was excited and started asking questions about the house.

In the middle of her conversation with Denise, the phone began making weird static sounds like it was a bad connection and like Sara was about to lose signal. Out of Cellular Never Never Land, a deep male voice took over the waves saying forcefully, "Don't call me! Don't call me!"

I watched as Sara's face grew pale. She said, "What?" The voice was gone and the telephone conversation with Denise began again with Sara telling Denise what just happened as I eavesdropped. Sara admitted after we left to feeling the old poo poo's presence although she did not actually see him—or smell him. Very likely, Sara's presence conjured up the old man.

That night, Maggie and I went to Sara's house to eat dinner. It had been a wonderful day, one that helped me visualize Sara's life growing up. After we finished eating, Sara got that look in her eyes.

"I can do this—now!"

"Do what?" I asked eyeing Sara.

"The story—Betsy's story. I'm ready. I can do this now."

"I need my camcorder and my computer!" I jumped up ready to run to the car and grab my gear knowing this was it—Sara was about to bust the legend wide open—or confirm what had already been written! The problem was my car was not outside. I had ridden with Sara, and my camcorder and computer were twenty minutes away at the motel. Sara's sister Jodie and Maggie jumped in Jodie's car and headed for the camcorder and computer while Sara and I gathered our thoughts and Sara's notebooks and got ready. An hour and a half later, Sara's disclosures were finished. All of a sudden, all of her experiences in Mississippi and Tennessee had come together and made sense. New answers were about to be disclosed and some old answers would be confirmed.

"What do we do now?" Sara asked.

"I will finish writing the book and we will disclose what you have seen, heard, and felt and you will tell Betsy's story just as it has been given to you." To me, the pathway was clear but Sara had one main concern.

"Should we tell Bob?" She asked. "It's his family's story, and I hate for the book to come out and shock him."

"I agree." I was not sure it was what I really wanted to do, but I knew Sara, sweet, kindhearted Sara, was right. I immediately made plans for a trip back to Adams the next week. Sara had become Facebook friends with Bob's daughter Anne Rickman who was very interested in what information Sara was getting about her ancestors.

Sara told Anne she had gotten much from visions and messages and that we would be coming to Adams soon to disclose all to Bob and Tim. Both men had been so supportive in our efforts to get Betsy's story and they deserved to know. And both believed in Sara. As Tim Hensen told me later, "I was so drawn to Sara. She is such a sweet, humble person, and I was amazed at what she came up with, things she could not have known."

On that first trip to Adams, Tim had been "blown away" as he said, by Sara and the information she had come up with as we walked over the Bell farm, visited the graves of John and Lucy Bell as well as other cemeteries, walked through Bellwood, with Sara literally feeling her way as she went. Concerning that first trip when I called Tim and told him I was bringing a "psychic" of sorts and that she was the "real deal", he had been skeptical just as I had been.

"I've lost count of the number of psychics and mediums who have come to Adams trying to sense something. They all ask me too many questions, and I always tell them, 'If I have to give you the information, you are not what you say you are.'" Tim always speaks what is on his mind and that is one of his qualities I appreciate most.

As we walked through each site, Sara called out names and events from almost two hundred years ago, information she did not have in her schema. Tim stood in the background, grinning from ear to ear and shaking his head. He was highly impressed, and just like me, he liked this young woman even though he had just met her. Bob ate lunch with us that day, and I could tell Bob had a positive feeling about Sara, probably sensing Tim's acceptance and general liking of her.

I mentioned to Bob how Sara had seen the girl in white, and Bob told about her following him and being seen by a local who was sensitive to spirits. Sara looked at Bob and said, "Well if it makes you feel better, I don't see her with you now."

Two weeks later, Sara and I were heading to Adams for our second visit, and this time we were staying in one of Bob's beautiful cabins out on Bell Bottom Farm. To make our visit even better, Sara's friend Anne Rickman, Bob's daughter, and her husband Michael were staying with us at the cabin.

Here we were in a magnificent family lodge, in the midst of beautifully groomed Bell farmland, surrounded by tobacco land and history. We were not on the original John Bell farm, but we were close enough, especially being the guests of John Bell's descendants. I knew Sara would be able to hear, see, and feel waves of the past in this awe-inspiring setting.

Late that night, Sara sat disclosing what had been presented to her from beyond the graves of Bob and Anne's ancestors. I filmed Sara as she told Bob about her gift and how she had been able to receive messages from those passed since she was three years old and how she had recently gone public. She told them how she acknowledged her gift and now offered her services to those who wanted to reach a loved one who had passed to see if they had messages for them. Then she got to the business at hand, the Bell Witch Legend.

Sara began to read through the disclosures I had transcribed from that night at her home and stopped periodically to explain how she saw the events. Bob seemed grateful for Sara's telling, the precursor to the book soon to be released. Bob followed Sara's disclosures by telling stories of his ancestors and about happenings in the twentieth and twenty-first centuries followed with many present-day events attributed to the spirit Kate. *(Sara's disclosures will be discussed in detail in the next chapter).* As Sara finished, Bob looked at her and said, "That makes more sense than any of the stories I've heard."

After Bob left, we settled in for our first night in this amazing cabin. Little, did we know!

The cabin is huge, more of a lodge than a cabin, with a basement level holding eleven beds. Sara and I picked the room with twin beds for our first night even though Sara had felt "something", perhaps a "ghostly greeter", in the basement when we first arrived. Anne and Michael would be in the master suite upstairs, two floors above us.

Earlier that night before Bob had come, and just for fun, we sat in one of the rooms in the basement with K-II meters and flashlights just to see if we could get any paranormal action. Sara immediately saw her bubbles and began playing with them with her finger. As she pulled one down on the bottom bunk, the K-II directly in the bubble's path shot to red continuously. Michael, Anne, and I knew Sara was pulling a bubble with her finger—a bubble invisible to the rest of us.

We went to bed in the wee hours that night, but Sara had a

hard time getting to sleep. Bubbles were everywhere in most of the downstairs, something Sara viewed in a positive light since they had been her security ever since she was a child, but it was not bubbles she saw on the ceiling in our room.

My eyes, tired from hours of driving and from the clock hands moving to 3:00 A.M. too quickly, shut as soon as my head hit the pillow, but Sara's eyes remained open, glued to the ceiling. As my mind tried to shut down, it kept sensing interference as a light darted around on the ceiling.

"Don't you see it, Sue?"

I peeped through tiny slits in my eyes and watched as Sara's flashlight on her phone bounced beams all around the ceiling.

"I don't see anything, Sara." I closed my eyes again trying to ignore the flashes of light above me and then felt guilty for not being sensitive to Sara's discomfort. "What do you see, Sara?"

"A black mass of something with little spiny things branching out from it."

"Um! Sounds like ectoplasm," I said wryly, as I turned my head toward the wall and closed my eyes. Ectoplasm is a ghostly substance thought to be a spirit trying to manifest. I hoped Sara did not know what ectoplasm was. Unfortunately, she did, and I only made things worse.

Sara was finally able to go to sleep after submerging her head under her covers where she could no longer see the ceiling. The next morning, she announced she would not be sleeping in the basement tonight. We decided we would sleep on the two comfy sofas in the beautiful main room with the huge stone fireplace, but by bedtime, we had changed our sleeping arrangements again.

The next day, Tim went with us again, and we revisited some of the places we had gone on the first trip as well as a few new places. Sara got no new messages but confirmed Andrew Jackson had been to the Bell farm.

Another reading she got came from Bellwood, a beautifully landscaped place of rest for many of the original Bell family members plus Bells from the twentieth and twentieth-first centuries. Sara had no clue what Bellwood was but started writing in her notebook. She wrote Clarence, Clarence, Sara Elizabeth, and Ada (?), but she had no clue why these names came to her. When we pulled up at the cemetery, Sara said, "Bellwood is a cemetery? Well, let's look for these names." She made one trek through the tombstones and found Clarence beside another Clarence with Sara Elizabeth not far away but then had to go to the other side searching for Ada with a question mark. There she was— Ada with no information beside or under her name. Ada is still alive; thus the question mark!

Bob visited that night, and we stayed up late listening to stories about Bob's dad Carney and the practical jokes he played. We had set out flashlights and K-II meters just for fun before Bob's arrival since we were in a Bell dwelling. What a surprise when Bob sat down beside a flashlight and a beam of light shot in his direction! This was followed by two K-II meters on the coffee table registering red every few seconds. The funnier the story Bob told about his dad, the louder we laughed and the heavier the activity. With flashlights and meters going off like fireworks, Bob began wondering if his Pop "Hollywood", Carney Bell's nickname, was not still pulling pranks from his grave.

After Bob left, Anne told us her own ghost story, one that took place at the cabin.

Anne used the cabin when she was in high school as a place for a sleepover with some of her girlfriends. They were doing fine until they heard one of the many doors on the wraparound porch rattling as if someone were trying to get in. They knew all the doors and windows were locked, but they turned all the porch lights on just to be sure nothing was peeking in through the myriad of windows. The rattling continued, and the girls became so frightened, they ran upstairs and barricaded themselves in the master bedroom and pulled a dresser in front of the door.

The next morning they inched down the stairs, making their way into the kitchen where they were shocked to find all of their food had disappeared. The doors were still locked, but when they checked on the porch, they found footprints of a small person with a "size 5 or 6 shoe", trailing completely around the porch. Beside the footprints, it looked as if the small person had drug a wet rope with one long track marking its trail.

At bedtime (3:00 A.M.), Sara and I decided we would sleep in the game room upstairs next to the master bedroom where Anne and Michael were sleeping rather than on the wide-open great room below. Sara insisted I take the long sofa and she curled up on the short one. Not long after retiring, Sara wrapped up in her quilt and spread out on the floor in front of my long sofa. She claimed her legs were too uncomfortable on the short sofa, but I believe she just needed a grandmother protector close.

The next morning, I got up early, made coffee downstairs in the kitchen and set to work on my computer. Sara came down and we began talking about the previous night and how scared we were. I felt a little ridiculous, being a ghost hunter who has spent nights in old prisons closed for decades, haunted hotels including the Stanley in Estes Park Colorado, and even insane asylums but I didn't say anything. Sara was fairly new to the ghost-hunting scenario even though she had been around spirits since she was three.

Our plans for the next day were to head to the Bell Witch Cave before leaving Adams, and then we would head to the Thomas House in Red Boiling Springs for a seriously haunted night in the beautiful old Victorian hotel. Sara already had a notebook full of messages from those departed who had connections with the Thomas House.

Soon Anne and Michael joined us, and the four of us sat at the table drinking coffee and talking about Sara's visions concerning the Bell Witch.

"I just wish we knew who the woman hanging in the tree and at the cemetery was." I stated. "And what connection she has to the girl in white and maybe the little boy you saw in the creek."

"Maybe she will explain it to me in another vision." Sara was very capable of receiving more from this woman or the girl. I hoped it would be soon since I had a publisher waiting on this book to be finished.

"I'm sure there is information somewhere if we just knew where to look. Maybe I'll call some archeologists in Nashville next week and find out about the tribal peoples and pioneers who settled middle Tennessee in the 17ᵗʰ and 18ᵗʰ centuries." I knew this would be time consuming. It would be so much faster if Sara got the documentation from her own "information highway", one I trusted more than the Internet and so much quicker.

Sara was feeling comfortable now that it was daylight and went downstairs to take a shower. Anne, Michael, and I continued talking at the table just at the top of the stairs leading to the basement but left the door at the top of the stairs open just in case Sara got frightened. After what I thought had been plenty of time for a shower, I listened from the top of the stairs checking on Sara.

"She is taking a long shower." I remarked. "The shower is still running."

In the next few minutes, Sara yelled, "Anne! Come here!"

Anne headed down the stairs, and in a couple of minutes, Sara called again.

"Sue! Come here!"

When I got downstairs, Sara was out of the shower, fully dressed, hair blown dry and styled, and her makeup on. I wondered how in the world she did all that when the shower was still going only minutes before.

"You won't believe what just happened!" Sara is excited, bordering on hysterical.

"I was about to get dressed, still had my towel wrapped around me when I heard Anne at the door. She said, 'You won't believe it! We found the document telling about the girl!'"

Sara said she got excited and told Anne to go get it and bring it down so she could see it. When Anne did not come back, Sara texted her asking, "Where's the document? I want to see it." Anne still did not come back, so she called Anne down and asked her where the paper was. Anne told Sara, "I don't know what you're talking about." Then Anne got the text Sara had sent. Sara said it was a perfect imitation of Anne's voice.

This was certainly possible. Many times, I have heard spirits mimic people, including myself, and would swear it was that person speaking rather than a spirit—except the persons being imitated swore they did not say anything.

Who was the voice speaking to Sara? Was it the girl in the white dress telling us to look for a document or something explaining who she and the woman are? Will the imitator put this document in our hands or in our paths? I, for one, hope this is the case. If we find out who the girl in white is, we will also find out the identification of the woman in the long, dark green dress.

Later, while at the Thomas House, Sara and I showed Darrel and Cindy, our friends and fellow ghost hunters, the picture of the phantom woman at the cemetery. As I enlarged the picture, I showed them the boy and girl figures seen by Brenda in North Carolina. I had posted the picture on Facebook as a "Find the phantom" kind of game with a discussion of matrixes (seeing shapes within other forms and patterns not related). Brenda had called me immediately and told me there were children in the picture also and directed me to the girl to the left of the tree.

"Oh, my gosh!" Sara put her eyes close to the computer screen. "Do you see what's in the girl's hand? She is not wearing white, but this has to be the girl, maybe with a black cloak on." Sara moved her eyes closer to the screen. "Look! She's holding a rope!"

Who was this phantom woman and this girl who seemed to be everywhere Betsy had been—or were they following Sara? Were they possibly protecting Betsy from Kate's return? Or were they trying to lead Sara to the truth about the Bell Witch? Either way, there was much yet to be disclosed.

Later, as I looked over Sara's notes from Adams, my mind became mired down in the muck and sadness of Betsy's life. Concerning the identity of Kate the entity, I answered the question I asked earlier: What was Kate? A ghost? A witch? A poltergeist? An angel? A demon? Following is my answer:

1) Ghost? Not a chance! Way too indulgent for Kate!

2) Poltergiest? Well, Kate was a mover and a shaker, and Betsy had just reached puberty, the age when poltergeist activity usually begins. But even the term poltergeist offers too much leniency for such atrocious acts of violence!

Girl holds white rope…to left of phantom woman…boy peeks
from behind tree to right of woman

3) Witch? Maybe, but she did a heck of a lot more than twitch her nose and boil vile stuff in a cauldron!

4) Angel? Never! Regardless of how many hymns sung, sermons repeated word for word, Bible passages quoted, or grapes dropped from the ceiling for Lucy Bell when she was sick, the fact remains—Kate was pure evil! She was NOT sent from God, and she was NOT an angel.

4) Demon? You bet your sweet biffy! In the summer of 1819, two young men from Alabama visited the John Bell home ready to be mesmerized by this wonderful angel who was making news all over the frontier. However, once getting to the Bell farm, they left much earlier than planned. Later a letter was received saying the boys "went to John Bell's to see the angel. It was no angel! It was the

devil!" Kate was both directly and indirectly the culprit responsible for ruining three Bell family members' lives—these three more than the rest of the family put together, with no hope of correcting these atrocities or letting them be forgotten—ever!

For those of you who know the legend well, you are now counting on your fingers: index finger for John Bell; middle finger for Betsy; ring finger for _____?

Who was the number three member of the Bell family whose life was ruined by Kate, or whatever cursed the Bells? Some of the real story should be told by Betsy Bell, the person whose life was impacted the most by it. But first, Sara's disclosure as she gave it to Bob Bell that night in his cabin—disclosures based on messages from the graves in Adams, Tennessee and Long Branch Cemetery in Yalobusha County, Mississippi, and any place they decided to speak to Sara. Here are some headliners for what you are about to read in the next two chapters, some headliners you might recognize as old theories—somewhat:

1) Bell Land Cursed! (*The land was cursed, not the Bell family, at least not inherently*).
2) Tooth Belonging in Indian Burial Ground is Desecrated Causing a Curse! (*Sound familiar? Yep, the old loose tooth under the porch story was true, even though Kate laughed hysterically telling John Bell it was a joke on him after he had the whole ground dug up and sifted.*)
3) The Sexual Abuse Theory Proves True! (*Betsy will tell this part*).

Now, here is the Bell Witch Legend as told *Through the Eyes of Angel Leigh*.

Chapter Twenty-Three

Sara's Disclosures

In this chapter, Sara's notes from that first trip to Adams, Tennessee, and the second trip will be discussed as they relate to the whole disclosure Sara will make. *(Some of Sara's most important notes will be shown in the appendices).* Remember, Sara had very little information about the Bell Witch Legend when she went to Adams that first time. This was intentional; it is how Sara operates.

During the first three visits to the cemetery in Mississippi, Sara got "sexual abuse" in the John Bell home, but her messages fell short of identifying the victim or the victimizer. Sara also kept hearing a female voice saying, "Chloe did it", but what Chloe did was left to conjecture.

Sara's notes are brief, written in a hurry, and are best deciphered by her. In this chapter, Sara will explain her notes in detail just as the messages were given to her. As Sara sat at the dining room table of her home in south Mississippi, she flipped through her notes beginning at the first and told the story just as she received it, whether it made sense to her or not. As she spoke, Maggie, my granddaughter, filmed her with my camcorder while I sat at the computer transcribing.

The following are all of Sara's disclosures based on notes transcribed that night on August 7, 2015, beginning at 9:05 P.M. at Sara's home in South Mississippi. Some information came to Sara while she was making her disclosures. No additions or subtractions have been made to Sara's telling, but it has been put in narrative form in historical order by myself as the author for easier understanding by readers. Quotation marks designate Sara's exact words.

Disclosures

When the Bells moved to what would be their farm in Adams, Tennessee, the land had a protection on it, a curse, placed there by a tribal people, "a known tribe" who lived there.

"I'll say Indians; if not, they were tribal like Indians. They know people can come in there, kill, and take the land" so they protect it. They did a chant with pebbles wrapped in white cloth and buried them under a trunk of a tree," and they "put it on the edge of the property all around the land as well. The Bells came along—wrong place, wrong time."

"There was a powerful spell cast on the land." Bad things began happening on the Bell farm starting on the outside, but then something happened later that made it go inside the Bell home. The Indians buried important things on the land, and they buried their dead making it sacred. Building on the land "disturbed the land" and the curse became active. Strange things began to be seen, and this was the beginning of the curse taking its effect on the Bells. One time, a black dog was found with its entrails pulled out.

The black dog story is heard again at the Thomas House. Darrell Cole told us about going inside one of the old out buildings that were still there on the farm a long time ago when people were still allowed to go on the John Bell farm. Darrell said it scared him to death because they found a dead black dog inside the building with all his guts out. *(In some of Sara's visions, and notes, she also mentions a strange dog and a strange bird just like were mentioned in the Charles Bailey Bell book but does not mention these this night when making the disclosure).*

Sara talks about the phantom lady in the long dark dress and the girl, about twelve or thirteen years old, who keeps showing up. Sara thinks they are connected to the land and to Betsy. She also talks about a young boy, the one in the brown pants and cap that she saw in the creek under the bridge on the old John Bell lands.

"A girl and a boy were there before the Bells came. They were part of the tribe. There was an older woman who was a healer and did a lot of chanting. She had a thing like a necklace with teeth on it. She would heal people by putting the necklace on the forehead of sick people, and they would sweat and get better. Something happened to her but there is a girl that follows people around. The girl was there before the Bells got there. This girl has long stringy black hair and wears a long white dress with cuffed long sleeves. She is not evil. The woman was hung in a tree and this was the healer. She had a dark dress on. The woman hanging is not evil. She was only there to protect her family and land before the Bells got there. I sense the woman was hung by water in Tennessee. I feel that she actually tried to protect Betsy in some ways. In my notes, I put 'near water, creek, hanging, no evil.' She was doing what she thought was right. Betsy could see her."

At one point, Sara told us she felt Betsy was sensitive like she is and could see things the other family members could not.

Sara confirms the woman is the phantom lady from Long Branch Cemetery, and she had her hair up on top of her head and was dressed either in a dark green or a black dress. The woman is white, not Indian.

Sara continues to see the girl in white even as this is being written. While writing about the girl, I called Sara to get a good description of the girl. In my mind, I had her looking like a sketch in the earlier books, a sketch supposed to be Betsy.

This is also the description given to me by a friend Mandy Mills-Beard who about ten years ago, visited the "Bell Witch Grave" with a friend and saw an apparition Mandy described as "a young woman dressed in a long white dress with long sleeves." The apparition Mandy and her friend both saw had "long dark curly hair with a band around the top made of flowers."

Betsy did not have dark hair like the girl described by Ingram, or the girl described by Mandy and Sara. Betsy's hair was blonde. But never would I try to discredit any apparitions seen at Long Branch Cemetery, not after photographing the phantom woman and the girl with a rope!

Here is the description of the girl in white as she has appeared to Sara many times, and how she still appears:

"She has long black hair that is stringy, not crinkly but completely straight and parted in the middle. It hangs down long across her chest but not to her waist and looks like she's doesn't brush it. Her chin is pointy, very defined, and she has high cheekbones like an Indian. She likes to keep her hair in her face, but one time I saw her with her hair blowing in the wind and she was looking right at me. I'm pretty sure her eyes are brown. Her dress is not pure white but is kind of antique white; it's long and long sleeved with ruffles at her wrists. She's short, under five feet tall, and looks to be no older than thirteen. Her voice is quiet, but she's only said 'Hi' to me. She was barefooted and might be half white, half Indian although her skin is much lighter than an Indian. I've been thinking, not that this was a vision, but maybe this woman came to this tribe and maybe got with an Indian man, perhaps a chief even, and had a boy and a girl. That is just speculation though. Before the Bells were there, I could see this girl and the boy, about eight years old, walking to the creek. Later, I saw Betsy and her brother walking to the creek and that was when they saw the woman hanging."

Sara confirms this story told in both the Ingram book and the Charles Bailey Bell book, as well as modern day books on the Bell Witch Legend, but Betsy's is just a little different. Betsy was walking by a creek one day with ONE of her brothers when they spotted something green hanging in a tree ahead. Being curious, they continued until they got close enough to see it was a woman hanging from a limb. Being frightened by it, they turned and ran back up the trail but stopped and looked back when they were a safe distance away. When they turned, the woman had disappeared. Here are Sara's words:

"The older woman, was a healer and very good to her people. She was very respected around the tribe and could touch them and heal them. She could not bring her people back to life though. There was a girl and a boy; I don't know who they were but they were in the tribe. I feel this is the same woman in the dark dress I saw in the cemetery in Mississippi. The woman was not evil to her people. She was protective of the tribe, land, and children." Betsy saw her hanging in a tree first and then took her food (*later*) since she asked for it. This was a test for Betsy. It was not the woman causing all the stuff (*with the Bells*) but she did cast some spells to protect the land. "She was not the one making bottles fly off the counters and all that (*in the Bell house*). I hear a lot of chanting and rattling—could be the pebbles in this thing rattling."

"There was something to do with this tooth. I see digging up things. They found part of a bone with a tooth in it. The bone, tooth, whatever was dug up and was brought inside. The house is gone now, but the tooth is still up under the ground where the house was. When they did that, it cursed the Bell family. It wasn't the woman that cursed the Bells. It was them digging up stuff, disturbing it, and that was what cursed the Bells. It was the tooth from the tribe, but nobody has it now. It is not in the museum. But the pebbles and stuff are still (*buried*) on the edge of the property and under the trunk of a tree. I feel the tree is still there and is important.

"I would be scared to go dig because the graves are there, and they (*people digging*) don't know about the tribe. They might find something they don't want to find, and the curse will be on their family. It sounds crazy, but occurrences have happened. The woman in the cemetery (*in Mississippi*) was the woman from Tennessee who was hanging in the tree. She was there for Betsy but also for the land. She can be either place.

"It's not KB, the neighbor. No. It's the woman from the tree. There is a spirit protecting the land and is a holy person over the tribe. Bones or a tooth is dug up and that made them mad and started the curse. Whoever touches this—they just got cursed! A different spirit was there who harassed the Bells after the bone was dug up, and it caused all the physical abuse and harassment. The marks (*on Betsy*), did not all come from the spirit; some of it came about because of sexual abuse. Betsy sometimes screamed and acted like it was the spirit to stop the sexual abuse."

Sara believes the teeth of the tribal people were considered sacred. During the session, Sara received two slave names, Anica and Harry. I knew Anica was probably Anky but had never heard of Harry. These two slaves were somehow involved with the tooth incident that was so devastating to the Bells. Even though it may not make sense, I believe it is important to show you how Sara explains her visions as they happen.

"Anica is coming back. She is a slave. She separated from Chloe who went one way and Anica goes another. Harry is coming up, too." At this point Sara asked me, "Did somebody lose a tooth?" She then continues as if she is seeing these questions connected to a vision about a tooth.

"Whose looking for a tooth? Be careful with that tooth. Anica and tooth—I keep getting that. It's more than just a tooth. The healer (*the woman*) had a necklace with some of the teeth on it. It's a powerful tooth!

"This is what I'm seeing (*pant or long sigh by Sara*). It's a tribe. One dies. They take the teeth out…one or two…they pray over them and then bury them. When they die they celebrate and pray over it and that protects that person. It's Holy ground to them. The land washed out and somebody found it and it was holy to the land. A spell was cast over it. So I see a lot of dirt and someone digging. I see Culson…Culson…Culson (*thinking out loud trying to come up with a C name*) digging in dirt. 'Hey, look what I found!' This had a protection over it. They took it and disrespected the tribe and the thing they took.

"Regardless of the tooth, tribe, anything and them moving there, things were gonna happen, especially to John because it was his choice to move there. That is why he died. He got sick before then with the spell on the land. Whoever brought something back from the dirt…it had a spell on it. Everybody buried there had a protection on them. Then disturbances started on the inside. It got physically painful for them." Sara pauses and then adds one statement.

"I think Drewry (*Betsy's older brother*) had something to do with digging up something."

Note: In most of the books written on the Bell Witch, the story of the "Lost Tooth" can be found. According to these, a friend of Drewry named Corban Hall convinced Drewry to go with him and dig in an Indian mound looking for relics. All they found was a jawbone that they brought back to the Bell house. Corban supposedly threw the jawbone against the house breaking out a tooth that fell through a crack in the porch. John Bell, when he saw what the boys had done, reprimanded them and had one of the field hands take the jawbone back and bury it. Could the C word Sara kept coming up with "Culson…Culson…Culson" have been "Corban?" Kate, the spirit, later implied to John Bell, this lost tooth had caused the curse. After John Bell had the grounds dug up and sifted looking for the tooth without finding it, Kate laughed boisterously saying, "It was all a joke on old Jack Bell!"

But was it a joke?

Two mysteries that remain unsolved about the Bell Witch story are: Who killed John Bell? And was Betsy sexually abused? These questions were answered, not by Sara, but through messages she received from Chloe and Betsy.

Who killed John Bell?

Many theories and stories are written about who killed John Bell. Kate's admission is probably the most widely accepted version. According to Ingram's book, John Bell had taken to his bed finally after months of trying to attend to his farm and duties while seriously ill. The story goes, the medicine cabinet was full of medicines left by the doctor, but on the morning of December 19, 1820, John Bell did not awaken at his usual hour and the doctor was called. On December 20, 1820, John Bell died. When a smoking medicine vial was found in the medicine cabinet, it was determined John Bell had been poisoned. Someone put a drop on a cat's tongue, and immediately the cat rolled over and died. Kate took credit laughing and exclaiming with joy, "I put it there and gave Old Jack a big dose out of it last night while he was asleep which fixed him!"

Even with this account based on the journal of Richard Williams Bell, much speculation was still to come, and once again poor Betsy was accused by many of poisoning her father. She had even been accused of being the one to cause the black magic that surrounded Kate, the witch. But what do the souls from beyond say? In Sara's words…

"The first thing I heard at the cemetery (*Long Branch*) and on my visits there was 'Chloe did it!' Chloe poisoned John, not KB.

Chloe did prayer chants. Betsy called Chloe 'Mammy.' Chloe was more of a mom to Betsy so she called Chloe Mammy. Betsy felt it was not forsaking her mama to call Chloe Mammy. I keep getting Chloe killed someone with the help of someone. Betsy did not kill her dad. Chloe did it. 'Chloe did it' was the first thing I caught, and I kept getting it. I said, 'Chloe, are you there?' She said, 'I'm here.'"

Many times in her notes, Sara used Kate and the eccentric neighbor KB interchangeably. I do not know what this means. Could Kate saying she was old Kate Batts' witch have been the truth? Sara said of Kate Batts in her disclosure, "KB, I feel was very mean but heartbroken." According to many sources, Kate Batts and John Bell had many disagreements, but in actuality Kate Batts was related to Lucy Bell. Did Kate Batts have anything to do with what happened to John Bell? This remains unanswered, but Chloe poisoned John Bell. Sara did say someone helped Chloe, but she never was given the identification of the person. Sara is sure Betsy had nothing to do with it. Sara is also sure of one other thing…

Was Betsy sexually abused?

In Sara's words:

"I'm not one hundred percent sure of why Betsy was attacked, but she was sexually abused. Chloe knew about it. She tried to protect Betsy and she could also do spells. It was in her family. She would do chants over Betsy trying to protect her from being attacked and from being sexually abused. The marks did not all come from the spirit. Some were from sexual abuse. The spirit who harassed the Bells after the bone was dug up caused all the physical abuse and harassment. There would be times Betsy screamed and acted like it was the spirit. She did this to keep from being sexually abused. Her parents would come up there.

"Betsy had a baby from being sexually abused. Betsy got pregnant but nobody could know. Not even a doctor was allowed to come there. Nobody could know. Betsy was either 7 months pregnant or more but the baby died either before or right after birth. Chloe put the cloth in the water and sprinkled/rubbed it over the baby's stomach like baptizing it. I could hear a baby crying at the cemetery—one little cry. The baby had no tombstone, no funeral, and was buried without a proper burial and never to be spoken of. Betsy was older than ten but not like seventeen.

"In my other notes I put 10-13. Chloe would go to Betsy, rub her forehead, rub her head, and say a protection prayer. John Sr. ran Joshua (*Gardner*) off. (*Betsy was pregnant and the family did not want anyone to see her*). Lucy felt sexual abuse was going on but prayed for it to stop. I'm not sure she knew who it was (*abusing Betsy*)."

After the night of the disclosure to Bob Bell, Anne Rickman, and Michael, Sara received a vision of the baby being buried at one corner of the outside of the cave, what is now known as the Bell Witch Cave. She did not get if Betsy gave birth in the cave or not, but it is a good summation.

So there you have the biggest bombshell presented to Sara by Betsy Bell and Chloe. Oh, I guess you want to know the identity of the abuser. Was it John Bell as some have theorized and as the movie *An American Haunting* played up at the end?

Betsy Bell, the older version, visited Sara, and Sara specifically asked Betsy, "Did your father sexually abuse you?" Betsy answered with a nod of her head that her father did NOT sexually abuse her. Sara then asked her who abused her sexually, and Betsy said his name.

Is this a cliffhanger? Yes. Betsy will disclose all in the next chapter. Be patient!

Chapter Twenty-Four

Betsy's Story

Yalobusha County, Mississippi
July 1888

    As daylight fades, Betsy Bell Powell sits in her rocker on the front porch of her daughter Eliza Jane's home in Mississippi. Now old and sickly, Betsy has been forced to live with her daughter for the last fifteen years. As shadows begin to play around her, Betsy's hand tenses on the arm of the chair and she ceases rocking. She cocks her ear, listening, but all she hears is the sound of crickets and tree frogs, an opus of southern night sounds. A full moon breaks through the oak branches illuminating the scene and relieving some but not all of the old woman's growing uneasiness. Her fears, old fears, never disappear completely as she remembers Kate and the trials and tribulations she was made to suffer as an adolescent girl just reaching maturity in Robertson County, Tennessee. Her thoughts carry her back to the year 1819 when she was thirteen-years-old and replay the horrors of that time. She shudders and her voice, though soft with age, echoes into the woods that surround her home with crackly clarity as if an ancient orator is speaking to a great and important audience giving her last speech.

Betsy

    My name is Elizabeth Bell Powell, and with God as my witness, I proclaim to the world I…AM…NOT…A…WITCH! I am eighty-two years old; I am ill and I am tired. Soon I will be well as I sit at the throne of Jesus and listen to the angels sing of glorious days ahead. I dream of being well, but I would gladly trade good health for one thing—to be unafraid.

Some say you get your childhood back in heaven if that was your best age on earth. I have no wish to replay my childhood unless this time, it can be lived with all wrongs against me righted—or better still, entirely wiped away from my existence and consciousness.

To walk again beside the creek with my brothers and feel no bitterness and no pain and to be void of vile memories still consuming me, this is what I want. Oh, to fall asleep at the home of my good friend Theny Thorne, giggling and taking turns tickling backs, talking little girl talk of boyfriends Joshua and Alex. If only I could go back to this time without fear of evil whispers in the dark, whispers that steal my childish joys crushing them into the Tennessee soil.

It is time. Time to tell what happened so long ago when our friends and neighbors along the Red River watched in awe as the spirit entertained and cajoled them. The spirit, "Our Family's Trouble" as Papa called it, took away my happiness, my security, my hope for a bright future with my love Joshua Gardner but it was not only the spirit who took away my youthful dreams.

It all started one spring day. Father sent two of our younger hands to clear the fields by the river. As they plowed, they turned up bones and became frightened. Papa knew there was a mound nearby but had no idea there were so many Indians buried on our land. He warned the field hands to be careful while clearing.

Brother Drew's friend Corban heard about the burial grounds and convinced Drew to go with him and dig in the mound hoping to find arrowheads and other Indian relics. Drew was easily swayed even though he knew Papa would disapprove. Corban and Drew brought home a jawbone of some poor native and treated it with the utmost disrespect, throwing it down on the porch and causing teeth to dislodge. When Papa found out, he scolded both Corban and Drew and had one of the field hands take the jawbone back and bury it. But not all of it was taken back. Drew kept one of the loose teeth as a souvenir.

Strange things began to happen on our farm after that,

maybe because of that. One day while Father was in the field, he saw an animal he could not identify. At first he thought it was a dog, but upon close scrutiny, it appeared to have a head like a rabbit. Father shot at it and being the expert marksman that he was, he was sure he had at least wounded it, but it was nowhere to be found. Later, while I was walking with Drew enjoying our beautiful rolling landscape as we often did, we came upon a bird of magnificent size, much bigger than a turkey and unlike anything we had ever seen. Drew, a good shot like Papa, shot at the bird but it, too, vanished. Another ghastly finding was when my brothers found a black dog on our land, its body disemboweled and left in the sun to rot and emit an awful stench.

But it was what I saw while walking beside the creek with one of my little brothers that gave me the eeriest feeling. We approached the big oak where we often sat in its shade seeking relief from the relentless summer sun. I had the idea to dangle our feet in the cool creek water but as we came closer, we saw something dark green hanging from a limb. Stopping and staring, we wondered if we should continue but our curiosity got the better of us and we inched closer. As we neared the tree, we thought it looked to be a young girl on the limb but upon closer inspection, we realized it was a small woman wearing a long dark green dress. She was hanging, a rope tied around her neck with her arms and legs hanging loosely as if the life had been drained out of them. I grabbed my little brother's hand and we fled. When a safe distance away, we stopped and turned to look one last time only to find the woman had disappeared. Perhaps, we would have gone back to see if we could see the woman again, but I heard our papa calling from a distance.

"Here, Daddy! We're over here!" I called back and grabbing my brother's hand, we fled to intersect with his voice. We did not tell what we had seen for a while fearful our papa would not let us return to the creek—if he believed us, that is.

Soon after, I saw the woman again in the orchard but she was alive. She spoke to me and asked if I had food, saying she was very hungry. Mother had read to us from the Bible how we must feed the hungry as Jesus did so I told the woman I would bring her food.

I returned home and sneaked a bit of bread and an apple into the pocket of my apron, but when I returned to the orchard, the woman was gone. I placed the food under the tree where I had seen her and when I returned later, the food was gone.

Big things, scary things began happening at our house. It started on the outside making knocking sounds and scratching at the doors but soon it moved inside making such awful racket I was certain a rat was gnawing at my bedposts. Then it began pulling our covers off, leaving my little brothers and me to shiver all night. If we tried to hold on to our covers, the invisible power would slap us and pull our hair. My little brothers were terrified, especially since Drew and John Jr. were away on the river and were not sleeping in the bed they shared in the boys' room upstairs, but at least Williams and Joel had each other. I was forced to sleep in a room alone after Sister Esther married and moved away. I tried to be brave for my little brothers but then the thing became violent, seeming to take all its vengeance out on me.

I screamed for Mother and Papa, but they could not stop the invisible monster from pulling my hair and slapping me. Many mornings I awoke with welts on my face and bruises on my body. I thought things would be better when my big brothers returned from their trip to New Orleans, flat boating on the Cumberland and Mississippi Rivers but I was wrong.

Drewry, the big brother I had always adored, returned from the river but John Jr. tarried longer. I loved the way my brother Drew, eleven years older than I, spoiled me with gifts from his trips. I had always loved cooking for Drew and doing other things just for him. He could hardly take his eyes off me and hugged me to him telling me I was the most beautiful girl in Tennessee and how all the boys would beat down the door wanting to be my beau. He would caress my long blonde hair and would even ask to brush it sometimes. Mammy Chloe did not like for Drew to brush my hair, but Mother thought it was sweet the way he fussed over me and would pry the brush from Chloe's black hand and hand it to Drew. Mammy would fold her arms and take a seat, watching and waiting for Drew to give her back the brush. Mammy was much more than my caretaker;

she was a second mother to me. I was the only one who called her Mammy but that is what she had always called herself to me.

I was now thirteen and the change had come upon me. My bosoms filled out too fast and I looked as old as my friend Theny even though she had reached her teens two years before me.

Drew changed, too. There was a look in his eyes, a haunting look, not the same as the sweet brother he had been before leaving on his river trip. Still, when the spirit came at night, he was first to come to my rescue even though it did no good. He, Mother, and Papa could only watch in horror until the spirit finished tormenting me. Then Mother would lie beside me, smoothing my tangled locks until I fell asleep in exhaustion.

One night, as I lay awake wondering if I would be able to sleep this night without my hair being pulled and my covers being torn off, I heard my door slowly open. It frightened me until I realized it was Drew. He put his finger to his lips shushing me and made his way to my bed. Pulling the covers back, he slipped in beside me and took me in his arms, smoothing my hair with his free hand.

"I will protect you sweet Elizabeth," Drew told me, and I did feel safe but then he changed. I cannot talk about what my brother did to me that night and many nights after. The only consolation to the embarrassment and pain was the spirit did not come into my room if Drew was there. I pleaded with my brother not to do this to me, but he assured me it was out of love and wanting to protect me from the evil spirit who now spoke to us and called herself Kate.

One night as Drew left my room, Papa, who had dragged his weak body up the stairs to check on me, met him outside my door. Drew nervously told him all was well and that he kept a good check on me. Each night I cried myself to sleep after my brother left. He told me I must never tell or Kate would make it worse on me. I believed him because Kate did not come the nights Drew came to me, and Kate never spoke of what Drew did, unlike the gossiping on our neighbors she was so fond of doing and always with an audience made up of church people.

Mammy knew. When she helped me wash my hair in my bath, she would sing her special hymns and would rub my forehead with a special mixture of herbs and sometimes with pebbles as she prayed over me in a language I did not understand.

"If you be fear of thangs, not jes Kate, you scream fo' yo' mama!" she told me.

I believe Papa knew about Drew. Papa would follow Drew with his eyes glaring. Drew removed himself from the family often and took refuge with Uncle Hank and the slaves in their quarters or with his friends.

The last night Drew slipped into my room, I remembered what Mammy had told me. Before he reached me, I sat up in bed and screamed as loud as I could. I yanked my nightcap off and mussed my hair and then tore the covers off my bed. Drew fled in alarm.

Soon after this, Drew left and went back to the river with John Jr., and while he was away, Kate came back and punished me with more fierceness than I had ever experienced. But she turned the full brunt of her torture on Papa who had become even weaker, his appetite fading. He could not chew for the sensation of having a stick turned sideways in his mouth and he writhed in pain. Kate laughed as she told us she would not leave until she had killed "Old Jack" as she called him.

Why Kate chose Papa and me to torture, we never found out but soon Papa took to his bed, never to rise. I, too, became deathly ill, having fainting spells and weakness mostly as each day drew to a close. My body was changing as well. I noticed Mother looking at me with a suspicious yet sorrowful look in her eyes but it was Mammy who told me what was wrong. I was with child, victimized by my brother Drew.

My pregnancy was never acknowledged in my home. No doctor was ever called to my attention, and Father would not allow any more visits by his own doctor. I stayed at home, not even allowed to go to church, supposedly helping to care for Papa. Papa ran Joshua Gardner away when he came to see me and even Theny was discouraged from coming. I feel sure Papa knew what Drew had done to me, but Papa turned his head from me each time I came to feed or tend him. He blamed me for what happened and stared scornfully at me as my body continued to change.

On December 20, 1820, Papa died, the victim of poisoning by Kate, or that is what she proclaimed as the family stood around Papa's deathbed. I secretly wondered if Mammy had taken it upon herself to punish Papa for not protecting me from Drew. I had once seen her remove a glass vial from the cabinet where the medicines were kept. Mammy prepared the meals in our home and that would make it easy for her to accomplish this deed.

The baby grew and often I would feel it kick in my belly but I hardly showed at all. I was stout but not robust and this helped to hide the transgression. My appetite left, as unbearable shame and fear overpowered me.

Mammy would sometimes take me for a walk in late evenings when there was no threat of meeting neighbors. It was on one of those evenings when we were walking by the cave where my friends and I had played not that long ago when pain hit me, becoming so intense I cried out. Mammy took me into the cave and helped me to lie down, and it was here that I gave birth to a premature baby too tiny to survive. This was a blessing for the poor bastard child born from incest and to me who would now never have to explain. Mammy, being a midwife for the slaves, pulled this tiny soul from my pain-wracked body as she chanted in the same language she always used when blessing me. She held the fragile infant up high while saying a prayer. It gave one short whimper and its soul passed from this horrid scene on to the lap of Jesus. Mammy tore another section from her petticoat where she had made rags and wet them with cave water to clean me and to help ease my pain. She had placed one cloth between my teeth to absorb my screams that would have otherwise echoed off the cave walls and threatened exposure. After dabbing the new cloth in water, she rubbed it over the baby's stomach and said a prayer, a simple baptizing for the tiny life no one would ever speak of.

Removing what was left of her petticoat, she wrapped the still infant in it and left the cave. I could hear her clearing away stones at one side of the entrance. With a stick, she dug a grave and placed the baby's body in it. With no proper burial, no scripture read other than what Mammy repeated from memory, the baby disappeared into obscurity, unnamed and unloved.

After Papa died, Kate gave us a reprieve. Drew found reasons to stay away from the house as much as possible and when he was there, he could not bring himself to even look at me. Mother tried to pet him as she always did before but he shirked away from her affections. Drew was eaten up with guilt over what he had done.

Our relationship would never be the same and neither would Drew. He never married but surrounded himself with people, mostly his Africans. I see that now as his own self-inflicted punishment for what he had done to me. Theny told me the neighbors talked about Drew and how he was extremely fearful of Kate coming back. This made no sense to me since Drew was not the victim of Kate's mightiest torture. Years later, when Drew was on his own with farm land to tend, he took a woman, Caroline, a slave, and though he could not formally wed her, he took care of her and she bore him children. Drew became a successful farmer and built a big house for his slave family, but he did not take part in the social functions in the community.

After Father's death, Joshua came back to me and asked for my hand in marriage, to which Mother heartily gave her blessing. But this was not to be. Kate, who had been silent after taking credit for Papa's poisoning, began to once again harass me, this time screaming, "Betsy, don't marry Joshua Gardner; you will never be happy."

Fear set in, fear for Joshua and for myself, and I requested a release from our engagement. Joshua acquiesced and moved from the area. I never saw him again. Soon, I had a new suitor, my teacher Professor Powell, who was much older than I and who was newly widowed. We married with Mother's blessing.

"My life with Richard was basically happy although Richard suffered a stroke and became an invalid far too early in our marriage. He died when we had been married twenty-four years. I have outlived all of our children except for Eliza Jane and Permelia. Homeless, sick, and without funds, I now live with Eliza Jane and her husband ZYX in Mississippi.

And now I sit here an old woman in ill health waiting on a

brighter hereafter. Drew tried to make up to me for what he did by leaving me more money in his will than he left our other brothers and Sister Esther but it could never undo the harm done. He also tried to help me by returning a slave he had bought from Richard. Mammy once told me she felt Kate cursed Drew because of the tooth and caused the terrible change in him. I want to believe this but I still can never forgive his actions. I pray when I see Drew in heaven, if he is there, all can be forgotten and once again I will be the innocent sister he once doted on and showered with love and respect.

I have seen the woman from the tree and the orchard many times in my life. I've even seen her lately in Mississippi. She wears a necklace of teeth around her small neck and I wonder if they hold magical powers. I feel she is a healer and a protector and I am one of her charges. I believe she lived with the tribal people who settled our land first and was their healer. Once I saw her saying something over pebbles as she wrapped them in a cloth, reminding me of Chloe and her chants. I once found where she had buried some of these magical pebbles on a corner of Papa's land but I left them there undisturbed. Perhaps, she placed the curse on our land for the tribal people she served. The woman in the dark green dress tested me that day in the orchard by begging for food. I passed the test when I brought her sustenance. I have also seen a young dark haired girl in white but she never ages. I believe she is connected to the lady in green, possibly her daughter or granddaughter. The girl often follows my grandchildren but they don't seem to see her. One thing I know for sure, the woman and the girl are not evil. Perhaps, she feels some responsibility to me if she was the one who placed the curse on the land. Maybe that is why she followed me to Mississippi.

Sometimes I think I see Mammy Chloe, and I dream of her blessing me with her pretty pebbles. I sometimes hear her singing to me and can almost feel her arms around me hugging me. Mammy loved me and I loved Mammy. If she were allowed to watch over me, even from the grave, she would.

And what of Kate? Do I see her? The answer is no, but I will always be fearful of her return. She haunts me every minute of each day and night. I sleep facing the wall and am fortunate to have a grandchild always willing to sleep with me, on the outside of the bed.

If heaven is safe and without Kate, then heaven is where I long to be.

Moonlight fades as clouds shroud its light, leaving Betsy waiting for death. The legend will continue to be told and changed, new theories rising with the next wave of writers, historians, and moviemakers. But in this book, Betsy tells her story—from the grave and what has been seen and sensed through Angel Leigh.

The lady in green watches over the cemetery where Betsy sleeps. Who is she, and who is the young girl who follows her and others? Perhaps, Angel Leigh will receive more messages answering these questions and will be led to the document she was told about that last morning spent in the cabin built by a Bell descendant. Then again, perhaps mystery will always surround The Bell Witch.

Afterword

Yes, this is fiction, but it is fiction based on Sara's disclosures with a few holes filled in mostly from Ingram's and Charles Bailey Bell's books. Here is some theoretical evidence pointing to Drewry if you need more than Sara's disclosure:

1) Drewry and John Jr.'s last flatboat trip together to New Orleans was around 1819. I'm not sure if Drew made that trip or not but Alex Gunn and John, Jr. did. Both Drew and John Jr. still lived at home when their father died.

2) Drewry never married…remained a farmer and lived a secluded life socially, surrounding himself with his slaves. A few years after his father's death, he took a mulatto slave woman Caroline as his mistress and they had two children, a boy Bolin and a girl Cotney. Did Drewry banish himself from Red River society out of guilt? Did he fear the return of Kate and more punishment? (*Sara got all of the information about Drewry, including his name, his woman's name and the fact that Caroline bore him a son whose name started with a*

*B and a daughter whose name started with a C. Sara knew
Caroline was black).*

3) Drewry died in 1865, and in his will, he left $5 to each sibling
and their offspring, but he left $25 (five times as much) to
Elizabeth and her offspring.

4) Drewry feared the return of Kate all his life as did Betsy even
though he was not tormented as Betsy and the small boys
Richard Williams and Joel had been.

5) Esther married in July 1817, leaving Elizabeth in a room
alone upstairs. The boys shared the other room upstairs. In
the boys' room, Drew and John Jr. shared a bed and little
brothers Richard Williams and Joel shared one. John Jr.
went on a six-month trip to N.C. once and was gone at other
times as well, leaving Drew upstairs with little brothers who
probably slept soundly, especially since Kate did not bother
them on the nights their big brother went to Betsy's room.

6) Elizabeth was beautiful with long blonde hair and blue eyes
and every boy had his eyes on her. Drew was eleven years
older than Elizabeth—probably with raging hormones (*an
obvious conclusion*).

7) According to Ingram's book, "Elizabeth had fainting spells,
followed by prostration, characterized by shortness of breath
and smothering sensations, panting as it were for life, and
becoming entirely exhausted..." and this happened every
evening for a length of time. Ingram's book also described
Betsy saying, "She was a very stout girl" (64). Was Betsy
pregnant?

8) Drewry was with Corban Hall and helped dig up the tooth
that set the curse in motion. This tooth was important to the
tribe or people who lived on the land first. If they died and
were buried, the protection was placed over them. Drew, by
digging up the tooth, brought the curse upon himself and
this could be why he molested his sister. He was raised by
Christian parents and was not raised to be a child molester.
Kate told John Sr. the tooth caused the curse but later laughed
and said it was a joke after the ground under the porch was

dug up and sifted and no tooth found. But was it a joke?

9) Another time, Kate told John Sr. about buried treasure on the land and where it was. Kate specified Drewry had to be one of the ones digging for it, and the treasure had to be given to Betsy with James Johnston there to hold the treasure and make sure Betsy received it. Why the specifications involving Drew and Betsy? Kate also said this was a joke after a hole six feet deep was dug but no treasure found. Was Kate making Drew pay a penance for what he had done to Betsy, or was Kate mocking Drewry? Was it an early clue given by Kate to John Sr.? These questions remain unanswered.

Chapter Twenty-Five

A Never-ending Life

This book is written about Sara, a young mother of twenty-nine at the time of this writing, who has a gift from God. It is Sara's story first and foremost. Betsy's story is but an offshoot, another soul getting to tell her story and make her peace through Sara.

Is what's told between these covers true? As the author and as Sara's friend who believes in her gift one hundred percent, I declare it to be true. But witnesses' declarations are only as good as those who read the accounts and are willing to let themselves believe. I am a witness for Sara as are others mentioned in this book.

Sara has earned the right to be believed and to be respected as she uses her gift for others. She was forced to bear the anxiety and the silencing without any pretense of understanding from both family members and friends as she grew from a toddler to an adult. With no one to turn to, she prayed, "God please take this away from me!" But God had bigger plans for Sara, and finally, after seeing the peace she brought to her grandfather and her own father by telling them what would happen after death, she saw the truth, the power, and the responsibility attached to her gift and she accepted it. Does she have peace after accepting her gift? Here are Sara's words:

"Sometimes, I can be with a large group of people, and everyone is laughing and talking, but I just feel different from them. I've always felt different. I wish I were normal in a way. When I talk about normal people, I just mean people who can't see spirits. But I feel more at peace when I'm helping souls. I've lost people in my life that I love because of what I am even though they never really knew me. Just my always being unavailable has caused me so many heartaches throughout my life. I have wished for so long I could tell the ones I care about what I do and show them my world. I guess now everyone will know, and I am relieved even though I'm unsure of what lies ahead. I wish I could let my friends see through my eyes, but I know most still wouldn't understand. I don't think many would unless they have let me help them. I have a strong bond with those I help, for each and every one of my clients. But I also feel a bond with the souls who come to me asking me to deliver their messages. The souls are as real to me as the people on this side. I can honestly say that a soul has never judged me. They have always accepted me and appreciated what I've done for them and their families. They, the souls, have never let me down. Sometimes, I feel happier and more content when I am with the souls who seek me."

Sara also knows God is always with her and she talks to Him constantly. She knows He will never let her down either.

What would it be like to be Angel Leigh? Imagine not being able to watch the news for fear of being bombarded with the unseen side of events and those responsible for the events reported. *(Sara says she gets anxiety attacks if she tries to watch the news).* Imagine being a teenager, a cheerleader on your way to a pep rally, and a boy brushes past you in the hall—a boy who was killed in car wreck a few days before. Imagine numbers flipping through your mind while sitting in church, demanding you write them down and later finding out they were the tag number of a kidnapper, a "pre Amber Alert" for a kidnapping that would end badly, and you didn't understand in time to stop it. Imagine seeing bubbles, ectoplasm, or just dead people in general everywhere you go and not being able to talk about it openly until now. The pressure of knowing would be unbearable.

Sara told me the other day, after seeing the dark cloaked figure she despises, she became depressed, fearful, and angry. She wanted to go outside and scream to the sky, "God, why did you give me this ability to see, but you won't give me the ability to stop it or at least provide advance warning and comfort?"

Then there's the wonderful side, the joy she brings to those of us fortunate enough to receive messages through her. Imagine each of these scenarios: being told as I was, "Your son is okay and is happy… God forgives suicide;" knowing your mother or grandmother who was so stooped in life, her back had to be broken for burial, now stands upright and can pick her tomatoes or dance the Charleston; being a parent or grandparent suffering over the loss of a child and being told, "Katie liked the balloons, and she has so many children to play with;" being told Grandpa Fred can chase chickens in heaven, he's laughing, and family surrounds him; the comfort in hearing from your own daughter as Randy Dulaney did, "When Papaw's time comes, your grandmother and brother are coming to pick him up in a Model T;" being told as Michael was, "your grandmother has held her great grandbaby Henry in heaven and rocked him before he will be handed to you in the delivery room."

Today as the first draft is being finished, Sara and I have had some major conversations on the phone since I am in Montana and she is in Mississippi. It was a good day for Sara as she relived some of the wonderful messages she has delivered and the joy she has felt at using her gift as God intended. I often try to tell people about some of Sara's miraculous adventures I have witnessed. Many want to hear more and get excited with me. But others, some very close, immediately offer every explanation they can think of to try to discredit her or they make up an excuse to leave the conversation and me. "I've got to go wash my truck," one person told me.

The other day I called Sara to get a good feel of how she sees Fred and all his UK family souls. She gave me a wonderful description, and I could truly visualize heaven, at least the "mansions" Jesus built especially for them.

Sara told me, "Sue, I wish you could see things through my eyes just for a few minutes so you would know how beautiful heaven is and how joyous these souls are when they speak to me from there."

I feel so blessed that God brought Sara into my life. My faith is so much stronger because of her. I have seen Sara's world through her eyes indirectly and felt her joy in describing it. But just for a minute, I would love to see and feel what heaven is really like—directly. I'd love to see my daddy pull a prank or see the twinkle in my sister Minnie's eyes as she laughs. I'd love to hear my Mam-ma call me Sudi. I'd love to see my little lost boys sitting on the lap of Jesus. I know I'd be just like Fred and say, "Whew! I'm in heaven!"

Sara's story is never ending. As long as there are souls who need messages delivered, she will be available. I think when her life on earth is finished, Sara will be a real angel, and she is probably in training at the moment. Her mission, her life, the good she does will have no end.

Angel Leigh is real!

Sara is real!

APPENDICES

Appendix A: Author's Notes and Acknowledgements

Appendix B: Photo Journal

Appendix C: Sara's Notes on Bell Witch Legend

Appendix A: Author's Notes and Acknowledgements

Cover Art: The cover art is by Sara's good friend Jessica Kell (jakthegreenfox@gmail.com) who is a professional artist. Jessica captured the very essence of Sarah, her dominant eye that sometimes holds images. In the cover picture, one of Sara's visions comes through, one she has seen often since starting this book. Sara thinks it is the mysterious "girl in white" who follows people, especially her. If only the girl would lead Sara to the document that would identify her and the woman in the dark green dress. Then again, maybe that is just what she is doing! *(In the cover art, Sara sees a profile of the girl in the gray area to the right of her pupil).*

Mysterious Happenings: Since beginning this book, many strange things have happened, especially as the book neared completion. Once I arrived in Montana where I could gaze at the Beartooth Mountains while I write, everything happened! First the sewer backed up, something that should have stopped my efforts but I didn't let it. I placed all my towels on the floor of the downstairs bath/laundry room, closed the door, left the vent running, and continued writing until the plumber could come.

On the day THE END was in sight *(a mirage)*, I could not keep my eyes open, something unusual for one who doesn't sleep much at night and never in the daytime. I would try to write and my eyes would close. The book was interrupted by two naps totaling two and a half hours. When I would talk to Sara on my cell phone, my wooden stairs would creak as if someone was walking down them, or I'd hear footsteps upstairs. But the worst was the foul order, worse than the sewage in the downstairs bathroom before it was repaired. This happened two times in areas not near plumbing or water. I was beginning to think the "stinky poo poo man" had taken up residence in my condo.

I put my cross necklace on, read my Bible, prayed, and then spoke aloud, demanding whatever was in my house to GET OUT NOW! Then I called my friend Gayle who told me to read Psalms 91 aloud as I walked through the condo. I had no sage to burn, but I did break off some spruce branches, singed a piece, and smudged the four corners of the condo praying as I went. I moved my computer to the table, set the spruce in water, took my wooden cross off the wall and laid it on top of my Bible, prayed every few minutes, and completed the main part of the book at 1:00 a.m. with no more problems—that day.

The day I was supposed to leave for Mississippi, I discovered the wrong manuscript had been sent to my publisher—an old copy that had been put in my trash; yet it was mysteriously sent, replacing the one clearly titled on my desktop. At 12:30 that night, I sent my publisher an email telling him what had happened. The next morning he emailed, "I received the new file at 12:30." He assured me everything was all right except—I didn't send a file with the email at 12:30. Once again, he had received an attachment with the same wrong copy, a copy I did NOT send! There is a phrase often used by those involved with the Bell Witch Legend: "Kate did it!" With Sara's prayers and reassurance that I am protected, I am sending this "Correct Copy" to Deron. With sage on my desk along with the wooden cross, my Bible, my cross necklace dangling over my heart, a deep sigh and a prayer, I will hit the send button—again!

The greatest thing to come out of writing *Through the Eyes of Angel Leigh* is the friendship and bond established between Sara and me. It is not often that a seventy-year-old woman and a twenty-nine-year-old woman become good friends but it happened. I keep telling Sara there is much left out of the book, things left for her to explain about her gift, but she will need these topics for the Today Show and all the other shows on which she will be invited to appear—not to mention the movie that will probably be made about this gifted and interesting young woman.

Acknowledgements: I would be remiss if I did not acknowledge those who helped make this book possible. The list is long but I'll try to be as brief as a writer can be. First, my thanks goes to Sara's family, especially to **Jodie and Denise** who took care of LeighAnna and Randyn while I took their mama away on trips to Adams and the Thomas House or to North Mississippi to talk to Betsy.

To all **those who gave us permission to use your readings** with Angel Leigh, I thank you. Your stories provided the credibility and validation so important for readers to see how gifted and blessed Sara is and to believe in her. A special thanks to **Randi** who made me see what was most important in the readings.

To **Tim Hensen**, our sincere thanks for all the information and the time you gave us so Sara could connect with those souls who had stories of their own to tell—many never told before. Tim, I doubt I'm through with you. You know I'm still addicted to Betsy Bell.

To **Bob Bell**, thank you for allowing us to stay in your beautiful lodge and yes, we would love to stay there again with or without the ectoplasm. Your support in this project was much needed and you never failed to give it. Maybe the next time Henry will be with us with his mom Anne Rickman and dad Michael. Now that would be fun!

A special thanks to the following people who gave me information, pictures, support and stories from the past:

Sharon Bell Hamilton, it all started with your invitation to witness the dowsing for unmarked graves at Long Branch Cemetery and you have been with me every step of the way. Thank you for being so willing to dig for information for me and even for the times you corrected me when I got the information on the Bells screwed up. You are a jewel of a friend!

Ralph and Pat Gordon, I thank you for the dowsing rods but I do expect you to train me to use them. Most of all, thank you for your summary of the Bell Witch legend, Ralph, and for your support in my efforts to learn Betsy's story firsthand.

Hilda Broome, you are a brave woman and a good friend! Thank you for not backing out after Sara gave you "too much information." I could not have filmed Sara in action in Adams, Tennessee without you being conjoined with her and holding that tape recorder where I wouldn't miss a thing—and in the rain! And thanks for joining me on visits to Betsy's. I look forward to many more.

Gayle Beard, what would I do without your editing? Well, my sentences would be too long with a run-on ever so often, not to mention overused commas! Oh, I guess that was a rhetorical question! You keep me on my toes and I thank you. Deron thanks you, too. (*Deron is my publisher*). Hilda and I will meet you at Betsy's and Nancy Jane's later.

Evelyn, Darrell, Cherry, and David Cole, thank you for again letting me include your beautiful hotel, The Thomas House, in yet another book. The grand old Victorian and the Cole family are a lot like Betsy Bell where I am concerned. I can never get enough!

Jim Hughes Turner, thank you for sharing your Great Grandmother Nancy Jane Wright Hughes with us. Nancy Jane would be so proud to know she had a great grandson with such a talent as a writer and such a willingness to share the family history. Why am I using past tense with Nancy Jane? She is proud of you! And she is known!

Brenda Abernathy, may you always see more than meets the eye! You are a joy to talk with on the phone as well as being a unique person. The little blonde boy thanks you, too. I am glad to call you my friend and hope to meet you soon. Until then, keep watching my posts—just in case!

To the souls that be and especially to Betsy, I hope we gave you the understanding you sought. May you rest in peace! And remember—Don't stay too long on this side when you visit! "Go back to the light!"

Last but not least, thank you, **Woody,** for not divorcing me. In the year you have been retired and finally at home, I have written three books. I love you. Get the fly rods ready and hook up the boat! It's time to fish!

Now as this book writing comes to an end, I can only think of one word to say…

"Whew!"

Dr. Sue

www.drsueclifton.com
See: Novels by Dr. Sue Clifton on Facebook

All of Dr. Sue's books may be purchased in eBooks and print on amazon.com.

Want to see more about Sara, Long Branch Cemetery, the Thomas House, and Betsy Bell? Check out these Links:

https://vimeo.com/134473629 Sara's Gift: The Yellow Flower, July 2015

Sara (Angel Leigh) explains how she accepted her God given gift of being a messenger for souls departed.

https://youtu.be/YAe4uFHhkG0 Sara at Long Branch Cemetery, July 9, 2015

https://youtu.be/3UsfkdxdiMM The Grave of Betsy Bell Powell Revisited, Feb. 8, 2014

https://youtu.be/HB6_YLal9bg Voices of Long Branch Cemetery, June 19, 2015 (Ralph Gordon dowses to locate unmarked graves)

https://youtu.be/R_nsBSwRSdQ Bob Bell Tells "Bell Witch" Stories with Modern Day Meaning

https://youtu.be/aPEnzNAFBlw Bell "Witch" of Yalobusha County Mississippi, June 16, 2014

https://youtu.be/PFMWzKDmG4c Mississippi Bell Witch Legend by Pat Fitzhugh, March 16, 2014

https://youtu.be/4vkoRjOS4OE The Best of the Thomas House 2012-2014

Appendix B: Photo Journal

Sara and Her Family

Sara Dulaney Pugh

Sara with her dad Randy

Sara with son Randyn

Sara with daughter LeighAnna
Sara's horse Midnight in background

Sara's mom Denise and Sister Jodie

Sister Brandy with Denise

Sara as a H.S. Cheerleader

Sara at 3, when it all began!

LeighAnna & Randyn with rescue animal

Sara is an animal lover. As such, she acts as a rescuer for local veterinarians and for any organizations or individuals that have animals who need tender loving care and a chance to survive. Sara teaches this love and care of animals to her children LeighAnna and Randyn.

Newest rescue animals: colt is named Spirit after play title in Adams, TN about the Bell Witch

RESEARCHING & INVESTIGATING
in MISSISSIPPI AND TENNESSEE

Looking for Unmarked Graves in Long Branch Cemetery, June 2015

Sharon Bell Hamilton & Dr. Sue

Ralph and Pat Gordon

Ralph Gordon, Professional Dowser and Author

INVESTIGATING IN
ADAMS, TENNESSEE

Sara with Bob Bell
Betsy Bell peeks over Sara's shoulder

Sara with Tim Hensen at Johnston Family Cemetery

Sara explains what she has received while
Hilda records and Tim grins in background
"blown away" by Sara

Sara gets a message in
the old cabin as Hilda
records...

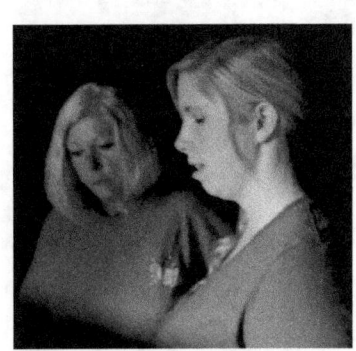

Sara at John Bell, Jr. house site

Sara takes notes

Cedar Hill, TN, The Thomas House and Back to Mississippi

Anne Rickman w/Henry, Michael and Sara

Darrell Cole, Sara & Cindy Smith
The Thomas House

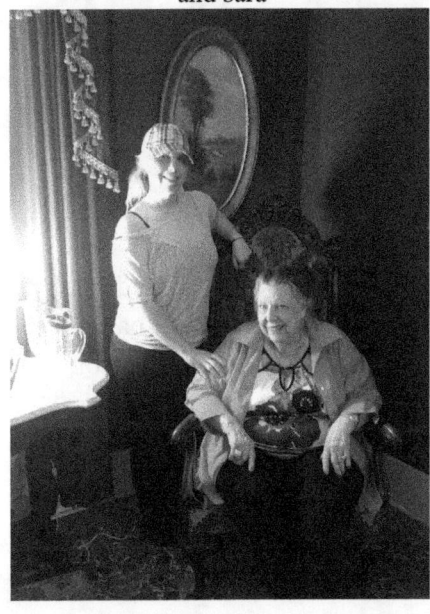

Sara and Evelyn Cole

Sara with David Cole

Sara and Dr. Sue
The Thomas House

Sara at Long Branch
Cemetery

Light follows Sara

Bell Witch Cave
Sara was creeped out by
this formation that looked
like a "Bird Person"

Park in Memory of Sisters Who Drowned

John Bell Farm, Adams, TN

Cabin on Bob Bell's Farm

Jessica Kell, Cover Artist
With Sara

Dr. Sue, Author, with Sara

Kate and Randal
Mississippi Paranormal Investigations

Appendix C: Some of Sara's Notes About the Bell Witch Legend

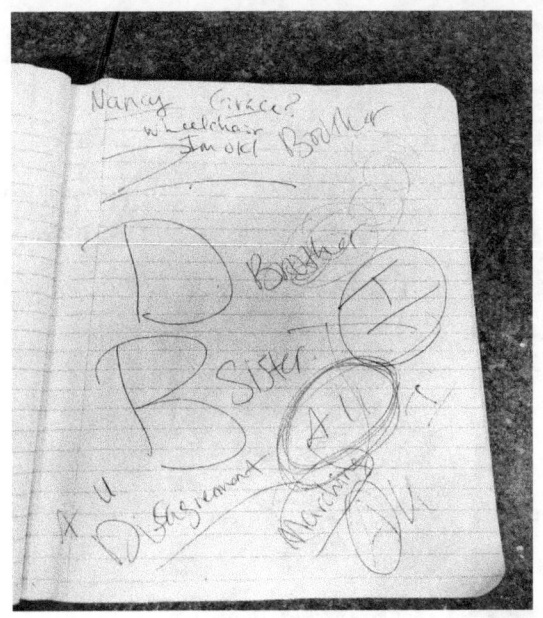

Bell Witch Legend: Disagreement over slaves;
Zadok, Drewery, Betsy

Bell Witch Legend: Dean; Powell; Kate Batts

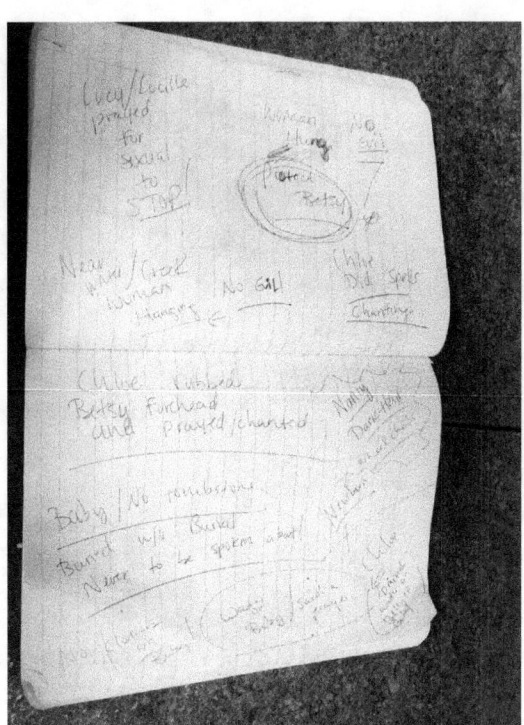

Woman hanging;
Sexual Abuse; Chloe
chants; Chloe baptizes
baby and buries it;
Sexual abuse of Betsy

Sexual Abuse of Betsy; Chloe killed John Bell

Lucy, Esther, Joshua and Betsy, Drewry's Woman & Children, Andrew Jackson Visit; Sara was pinched at 12:25 when gets KB, Kate Batts

Curse caused by tooth: baby buried by cave entrance

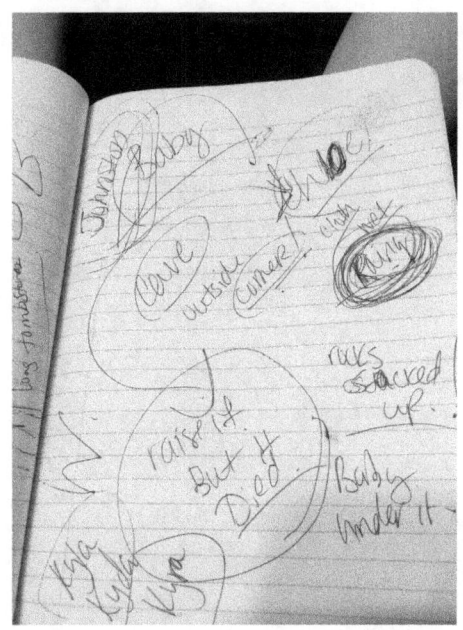

About the Author...

Dr. Sue Clifton is a retired principal and teacher, a fly fisher, a ghost hunter, and a published author. Dr. Sue, as she is known, can't remember a time when she did not write beginning with two plays published at age sixteen. Her writing career was placed on hold while she traveled the world with her husband Woody in his career as well as with her own career as a teacher and principal in Mississippi, Alaska, New Zealand, and on the Northern Cheyenne Reservation in Montana. The places Dr. Sue has lived provide rich background and settings for the novels she creates.

Dr. Sue now divides her time between Montana, Mississippi, and Arkansas and enjoys traveling with Woody as well as with her 5000-plus national fly fishing group, Sisters On the Fly. Dr. Sue loves all things vintage, including her 1950 camper "Spam I Am" and her 1951 Plymouth Savoy "Woodie 2."

Dr. Sue is the author of eight novels including three paranormal mysteries with Double Dragon Publishing and four in her Daughters of Parrish Oaks series with The Wild Rose Press, Inc.

Visit Dr. Sue at: http://www.drsueclifton.com

and

Novels by Dr. Sue Clifton on Facebook